THE SMELLY
LITTLE DOG

and other stories

Illustrated by
Edgar Hodges

World International Publishing Limited
Manchester

Published in Great Britain by World International
Publishing Limited,
An Egmont Company, Egmont House, PO Box 111,
Great Ducie Street,
Manchester M60 3BL.
Printed in Italy.

British Library Cataloguing in Publication Data
Blyton, Enid 1897–1968
The smelly little dog and other stories.
I. Title II. Series.
823.912 [J]

ISBN 0–7498–0315–0

Cover illustration by Robin Lawrie

Contents

Enid Blyton

Enid Blyton was born in London in 1897. Her childhood was spent in Beckenham, Kent, and as a child she began to write poems, stories and plays. She trained to be a teacher but she devoted her whole life to being a children's author. Her first book was a collection of poems for children, published in 1922. In 1926 she began to write a weekly magazine for children called *Sunny Stories*, and it was here that many of her most popular stories and characters first appeared. The magazine was immensely popular and in 1953 it became *The Enid Blyton Magazine*.

She wrote more than 600 books for children and many of her most popular series are still published all over the world. Her books have been translated into over 30 languages. Enid Blyton died in 1968.

The smelly little dog

The children rushed down on to the beach with their spades and buckets and boats. Mummy followed with the packets of sandwiches and a big bottle of lemonade. She signalled to the man who hired out deckchairs and he came hurrying up with one at once.

"There!" said Mummy, sitting down thankfully, for it was a long walk from their boarding house to the beach. "Now you've a whole day to play and paddle and swim, children. It's so hot today that you can get as wet as you like – the sun will soon dry you."

Joan, Fred and Betsy felt very happy. The things they would do! "Build an *enormous* castle with a moat round it full of water!" said Fred.

"And sail my boat on those little waves," said Joan.

"And take my teddy paddling with me," said little Betsy.

"And have ice-creams when the ice-cream man comes round!" said Mummy, laughing. "Oh – here's that little dog again! Go away, dog – you're smelly!"

"Mummy, he's quite a nice little dog," said Fred. "I know he looks very dirty, though he *does* go splashing in the sea quite a lot, and ought to be quite clean by now! And I'm sure his master doesn't give him enough to eat. He's so thin!"

"Get away from those packets of sandwiches, Dog," said Mummy, crossly, as the dog came sniffing round. "You're always hungry. Why doesn't your master feed you properly?"

The deckchair man stood nearby. He chased the little dog away. "Off with you! You don't belong to anyone, do you? You're a nasty little stray!"

"He's *not* nasty," said Betsy, at once. "He's got a nice face. I like him. I want him to play with me."

So the little dog played with them all the morning, though Mummy shooed him away as soon as he came near her and the sandwiches. He put his tail down then, and slunk away quietly.

Betsy shared her sandwiches with him when dinner-time came, and so did Fred and Joan. He seemed very, *very* hungry, but he was quite polite and didn't snap at all. He seemed to like Betsy best, and she cuddled him to her when she had finished her sandwiches.

"Betsy! You are NOT to cuddle that smelly little dog!" said Mummy, sharply. "Oh, I know he's friendly enough, but it's only your sandwiches he's after. Push him away. Go home, Dog, go home!"

The little dog ran off, and sat down, looking very sad. Nobody ever wanted him. He really was dirty and smelly, and very thin. He would certainly have gone home if he could – but he hadn't had a home since he was a puppy and had been left behind on the beach by a man who didn't want him. So how *could* he go home?

"Now," said Mummy, when all the biscuits and apples she had brought had been eaten, "you can go and buy a big ice-cream each from the ice-cream man up on the front, and bars of chocolate from the sweet shop. Take Fred's hand, Betsy."

The little dog went with them. He liked these children. They didn't throw stones at him, and call him horrid names as some children did. Perhaps he might have a lick at an ice-cream – the ice-cream man sometimes spilt some as he slapped it between the wafers.

When the children came back to the beach, their mother was fast asleep. "What shall we do?" asked Fred. "I think I'll go for a swim. Come on, Joanie."

Betsy looked sad. She couldn't swim

like the others. "I shall paddle," she said. "And I shall take my teddy bear too. He told me yesterday that he likes paddling."

"The things that bear says to you!" said Joan, laughing. "I shouldn't take him paddling, Betsy. He won't like getting his feet wet."

"He told me he did like it," said Betsy seriously. "He told me his feet were hot, like mine, and he wanted to feel the cold sea on them."

The others laughed and ran into the sea at top speed, plunging into the big waves. They were good swimmers. Betsy stood and watched them. "I can't swim, Teddy, and you can't either," she said. "But one day we'll be big enough!"

She walked her big bear down the sands to the edge of the waves, talking to him. The sea felt lovely and cool over her toes. She dabbled the bear's toes in too.

The little dog came and sat down at the edge of the sea and watched. He was afraid to go too near Betsy and the bear in case they didn't want him. He saw Joan and Fred quite far out, and gave a little bark as if to say, "Be careful now!"

But they were such good swimmers that they were quite safe. They were racing one another to the pier. Betsy watched them. "Let's go in a bit further, Teddy," she said, feeling very brave. "You're not afraid of the big waves, are you? I'm not either!"

So they went further in, the teddy bear getting wet right up to his neck! "Do you like it, Teddy?" said Betsy. "Yes, you do! Oh, look at this great big wave coming – hold my hand tight!"

The wave was really very big indeed. It curled over just as it reached Betsy and splashed right over her head. She sat down very suddenly indeed and let go of the bear's paw. In a trice the wave had taken him away from her into deeper water! There he went, turning over and over, his little brown body as wet as could be!

13

"Teddy! Come back! You'll be drowned!" shouted Betsy, getting up and wading after him. But, oh dear, another big wave came, and over she went again. Then, before she could get up, spluttering and frightened, another one broke right over her, and she disappeared under the water. The wave rolled her over into the sea when it ran back itself, and poor little Betsy couldn't even stand up!

Fred and Joan didn't see. They were too far away. Mummy didn't see either, because she was fast asleep. Nobody saw — except the smelly little dog. He stood up at once when he heard Betsy scream. Then he plunged into the waves and swam steadily out to her.

And at that very moment Mummy woke up! She sat up to see where the children were — and saw poor little Betsy being taken away by the waves! She screamed loudly and began to run down to the beach.

The little dog was almost up to Betsy.

Ah – there she was! He snapped at her swimsuit and got it between his teeth. Then he tried to swim towards the beach with her.

But she was very heavy for such a little dog. He panted and puffed, swallowing water – but he didn't let go of the swimsuit! No – he clung on to it for all he was worth! This was the little girl he liked. This was the little girl who always spoke kindly to him! She was in trouble, and there wasn't anyone but him to help her.

He dragged poor Betsy into shallower water, and then, just as he thought he simply couldn't hold on any longer, someone caught hold of Betsy and lifted her up.

It was her mother, who had waded out to her and the little dog! She waded back with Betsy, who was choking and spluttering and crying with fright. The little dog followed and sat down at a safe distance to watch.

"Darling! You shouldn't have gone

out so far!" said Mummy, cuddling poor frightened Betsy. "You might have been drowned. You would have been if that smelly little dog hadn't gone after you and tried to bring you back."

"I went after my teddy," said Betsy, crying. "He's still out there, Mummy. He'll drown. Oh, please get him for me."

"I can't bother about your teddy now," said Mummy, hugging her. "I'm only too glad *you* are safe!"

But *some*one bothered about her teddy – yes, the little dog! He heard what Betsy said, and quick as a flash he was in the sea again, swimming after the poor teddy, who was now so soaked with water that he was almost sinking! Only his little bear-nose could be seen!

The little dog caught hold of him and swam back at once. He laid the bear down on the sand beside Betsy, and then, as Fred and Joan came racing out of the water to find out what was happening, he went a little way away and sat down again. He was very, very glad he had been able to save the bear too, but he was sad to hear Betsy crying.

She soon stopped when she saw her teddy bear beside her. She took him up, soaking wet as he was, and hugged him to her. "That little dog saved you too," she said. "Mummy, isn't he a *good* little dog?"

"Very, *very* good," said Mummy, hugging Betsy again. "Fred – Joan – little Betsy was nearly drowned when she took her teddy into the water for a paddle. If it hadn't been for that little dog, who raced after her and got her out of the waves, she *would* have been drowned. Oh, Betsy – to think I was asleep too, and didn't know till almost too late!"

"Oh, you *good* little dog!" said Fred, turning to where the little creature sat, his head on one side, listening. He was very, very wet, but he didn't mind that at all. He was so very glad that the little girl he liked was smiling again.

"Mummy – I want to hug that little

dog," said Betsy. "Come here, Dog, come here!"

He ran up, his tail down, wondering if he was going to be scolded. But no – of course he wasn't! Betsy hugged him, Fred hugged him, and Joan too. And then Mummy patted him and spoke to him kindly.

"Little dog – you need a home. Would you like to come and live with us? We have an old kennel that you could have. I shall never, never forget what you did today, never! You are the best little dog in the world!"

Well, the dog couldn't believe his ears! He licked Mummy, he pranced round, and his tail wagged so fast that it could hardly be seen. Then he went and lay down beside Betsy, his head on her knee, as if to say, "I'm *your* dog. I belong to *you*!"

Betsy understood, of course. "Yes, you're *my* dog," she said. "I'll certainly share you with the others, but you belong to *me*. And I'm going to call you Splash because you splashed into the water to save me!"

And that was how Splash came to live with a little family of his own. You wouldn't know him now! He is spotlessly clean, gleaming black and white, his tail is always up, and he is quite plump!

I know all about him because one day I heard Betsy shouting "Splash! Splash!" when she called him to her. I asked her why he had such a strange name, and when she told me, I thought I really must tell *you* – and that is how this story came to be written!

You bad little dog

John and Freda took their little dog Wuff down to the sands with them. It was such a lovely beach for little dogs, as well as for children!

There was fine golden sand stretching right down to the very edge of the sea – and tiny waves to play in, and warm pools to bathe in. Wuff liked it as much as John and Freda did.

That morning the children had their spades with them. They meant to build the biggest castle on the beach – bigger even than Tom and Peter and Dick had built the week before. That one was so big that the sea just couldn't knock it all down, but left half of it for the next day.

21

Wuff wanted to build, too – but as his idea of building was to dig enormous holes and scatter the sand all over the place, John and Freda wouldn't let him help.

"No," they said. "You keep away today, Wuff. You're just being a nuisance. As soon as we get a heap built up you scrape a hole in it. That's not building!"

So Wuff went a little way away and sat down sadly to look at the two children building. Soon an old man came and sat down in a deckchair nearby. He opened his newspaper and began to read. He wasn't near the children, and they took no notice of him at all.

But Wuff was quite near him, sitting still, feeling rather bored. He suddenly smelt rather a nice smell. He got up and ambled round and about, sniffing at the sand. Ah – here was the smell!

Someone had left a bit of cake in the sand and Wuff felt that he really

22

must dig it up. So he began to scrape violently with his front paws. Up into the air went great showers of fine sand – and the old man found himself being covered from head to foot.

"Stop it," he growled to Wuff. But Wuff was too happy to hear. He was getting near that bit of cake! Up flew some more sand, and down it came on the old man's newspaper, making a little rattling noise.

The man jumped up in anger. He picked up some seaweed and threw it at Wuff. "Bad dog, you! Go away! They shouldn't allow dogs on the beach. I've always said so! Grrrrr!"

The seaweed hit Wuff and he yelped and ran off. He was frightened, too, when the man made the growling noise because it sounded like a big dog!

The children were very cross when they saw the old man throwing seaweed at Wuff and heard him shouting. "Just because Wuff threw some sand over him by mistake!" said Freda.

"You take that nasty little dog of yours away from this beach!" shouted the old man. "If he comes near me again he'll be sorry!"

Freda and John were upset. They left their castle half-finished, and Wuff left the hidden bit of cake, and they all went right to the other end of the beach. They began to build another castle, but it was dinner-time before they had done very much. They were very disappointed.

"Now the sea will be able to sweep away all we've done," said John. "The castle ought to be twice as high if there's to be any left when the tide goes out again."

They went home to dinner, Wuff dancing round their legs. The old man had gone, too. The deckchair was empty and the chair-man was just about to pile it with all the others, so that the sea wouldn't take it away when the tide came in.

Next morning the children went down to the beach again. Wuff went, too. The old man was there in his chair, and John and Freda decided not to go too near him.

"We really must work hard this morning," said John. "Granny is coming this afternoon and it would be lovely to show her a really magnificent castle, bigger than any on the beach."

"Wuff," said Wuff, quite agreeing.

"You go away till we've finished," said Freda to Wuff. "Look, take your ball and go over there to play with it. You aren't much good at castles, Wuff."

Wuff took his ball. But it was really very boring to play by himself, and he suddenly remembered the bit of cake he had smelt in the sand the day before. Suppose it was still there? He could perhaps find it this time. He began to run about, sniffing, to see if he could smell it again.

He came near to the old man and stopped. Why, here was the man who growled like a dog and threw seaweed at him! He'd better be careful or he might be hit by another piece of soggy seaweed.

The old man sat quite still. He didn't speak or move. Wuff sniffed the air. Was he asleep? When people were asleep they didn't shout or throw things. He could look for that bit of cake if the old man was asleep.

He *was* asleep – fast asleep in the warm sun. His newspaper lay on his knee. The wind tugged at it, trying to get it.

Wuff began to scrape in the sand for the bit of cake. A few grains flew into the air and fell on the newspaper on the man's knee. He didn't stir at all. The wind suddenly blew strongly and the newspaper flapped hard. It flapped itself right off the man's knee on to the sand.

Wuff stopped burrowing and looked at it. Soon that newspaper would blow right away. He didn't know why people liked newspapers so much, but he knew they did. This one belonged to the old man. Did he want it? Would he mind if his paper blew right into the sea?

The children suddenly saw Wuff near the old man again. They called to him. "Wuff! Wuff! Come away from there! You know you got into trouble yesterday."

Then John saw the newspaper blowing away. "Look," he said, "the paper has blown off that man's knee. He must be asleep. There it goes! Oh, won't he be cross when he wakes up and finds that the sea has got it!"

"It will serve him right for throwing seaweed at Wuff," said Freda.

"There goes the paper – almost into that pool," said John. "Wuff – fetch it, then, fetch it, boy!"

Wuff raced after the paper and pounced on it just before it flew into the pool! The old man, awakened by the shouting, sat up and looked round to see what the noise was about.

He saw Wuff pouncing on his paper – and then the little black dog turned and ran all the way back to the old man with it and put it down by his feet, just as he did when he ran after a ball and took it back to the children.

"Why, you good, clever dog!" said the old man, patting him. "Fine dog, good dog! Who do you belong to?"

"He belongs to us," said John and Freda, coming up, astonished to find the man making such a fuss of Wuff.

"Well, he's a very clever dog," said the man, folding up his newspaper. "Not a bit like a horrid little dog I saw here yesterday, who threw sand all over me. Oh, he was a dreadful little thing!"

"Wuff!" said Wuff, trying to tell the man that yesterday's dog and today's were exactly the same. But the man didn't understand.

"I must buy a bone for this good dog," said the man. "Does he like bones?"

"Yes. But he likes ice-creams even better," said Freda.

"Well, well – what good taste he has!"

28

said the man, getting up. "Shall we all go and buy ice-creams? Come along, then."

They went to the ice-cream man and the old man bought four ice-creams, one for each of them and one for Wuff too, of course. Then he went down to look at the castle the children were building.

"I'd better help you with this," he said. "I can see you won't finish it if I don't. We'll make it the biggest one ever seen!"

They finished their ice-creams, Wuff too, and set to work. My goodness me, how the old man could dig! You should have seen that castle when it was finished. All the children on the beach came to admire it.

"Well, thank you very much indeed for the ice-creams and the digging," said John and Freda.

"I'll help you again tomorrow," said the man, smiling. "Goodbye – and goodbye, little dog. I'm glad you're not like the nasty little dog I shouted at yesterday!"

Off he went. The two children looked at one another. "Well! He may think Wuff is a different dog – but honestly *he's* a different man, too!" said John. "Who would have guessed he could be so nice?"

It *was* funny, wasn't it? What a good thing Wuff ran after his paper!

The little brownie house

Kim and Mickle were very worried. They were brownies who lived in a tree house like Josie, Click, and Bun – and now the woodman had come to chop down their tree.

"We shall have to move," said Kim. "And quickly too, or the tree will come down and all our furniture with it! Hurry, Mickle, and get it all out."

So the brownies took their furniture on their shoulders and piled it on the grass outside. There it stood, and there the brownies stood too, wondering where to go.

They borrowed a hand cart from Bonny the pixie and put the furniture on it, ready to wheel away. But there really seemed nowhere at all to go. There had been so many old trees cut down in the wood that many people had taken all the empty houses there were.

"There's not even a hole in a grassy bank we can have," said Kim. "At least, there's one – but the fox lives there, and he doesn't smell very nice."

"Oh, we can't go there," said Mickle. "We'd have to hold our noses!"

"Well, let's wheel our barrow round a bit and see if there's any empty house we can go to," said Kim. So, with the noise of the woodman's axe ringing in their ears, they wheeled their cart away, with their two little beds, their two little chairs, their table, cupboard, curtains and mats on it, looking rather sad.

They came at last to a high hedge. At the bottom was a gap, so they wheeled the barrow through – and there in a garden was a little empty house! It was painted brown, and had a big open doorway.

THE LITTLE BROWNIE HOUSE

"I say! Look at this!" cried Kim, running to it. "An empty house – just our size too! What about living here? There's nothing in the house at all, except some old straw."

"It's fine," said Mickle. "But it's rather a funny house, Kim – there's no door – and no window either!"

"Well, that doesn't matter, Mickle!" said Kim. "We can easily make a door, and just as easily make a window! Oh, Mickle – it will be fun living in this little house, won't it!"

Well, the two brownies moved in. The house was exactly right for them. They put in their beds, one on each side of the room, for the house had only the one room. "Our beds can do for sofas, in the daytime," said Kim.

They put the table in the middle, and the chairs beside it. They put the cupboard at the back, and spread the rugs on the floor. You can't think how lovely it all looked when it was done.

They had a tiny jam jar and Kim went

to fetch some daisies for it. He put the vase of daisies in the middle of the table.

Mickle put the clock on the cupboard and wound it up. Tick-tick-tock-tock! it went.

"There now," said Kim. "Flowers on the table – and a clock ticking. It's home, real home, isn't it?"

The brownies were very happy. The little house looked out on to a garden belonging to a big house built of brick. People lived there, and two children often came out of the house to play. But they never came to the brownies' house.

"It's a good thing our house is right at the bottom of the garden, where nobody ever comes," said Kim. "Now, Mickle – what about making a door? The rain came in yesterday and wet the carpet."

So the two brownies set about making a door. They found a nice piece of wood, and with their tools they made it just the right size for a door. They painted it blue, and hung it in the doorway with two little brass hinges. It opened and shut beautifully.

They put a knocker on it and made a slit for a letterbox. It did look nice.

"And now we'd better make two little windows," said Mickle. "When we have the door shut our house is very dark and stuffy. We will make a little window each side and find some glass to put in."

So they carved out two squares for windows, and found an old glass bottle by the garden frames. They cut two pieces of glass out of the bottle to the right size, and fitted them in. Then they cleaned the windows, and hung up blue curtains.

"Really, it looks simply lovely now!" said Kim. "The door is such a nice blue and the knocker shines so brightly, and the curtains at the window look so pretty. I think we ought to have a party."

"Yes, we ought," said Mickle. "But if we give a party, we must make cakes. And we can't bake cakes unless we have an oven and a chimney – and there isn't a chimney, you know."

So they made a chimney, and bought a nice little oven from the pixie down the way. They fixed it into the corner, and then lit a fire. The smoke went straight up the chimney and away into the garden. It was marvellous! The oven cooked beautifully, and what a delicious smell came from it the first time that the brownies cooked buns and cakes!

They sent out the invitations to the party. "Everyone will love our little house," said Kim. "They will think we are very, very lucky to have found it. I do wonder who it belonged to. We have never heard."

Now, on the day of the party, Kim and Mickle began to do a great cleaning and cooking. All the mats were shaken, the windows were cleaned, the knocker was polished, and the stove cooked cakes, buns, and biscuits without stopping. It was great fun.

And then something extraordinary

happened! A voice outside the house cried out, "Look at this! There's somebody living here!"

The brownies peeped out of the window and saw two children, a boy and girl, staring in the greatest astonishment at their house. "Goodness!" said Mickle. "Do you suppose it's *their* house, and they want to come back and live in it? Oh dear, I do hope they won't turn us out!"

"We'd better go and ask them," said Kim. But before he could do that, somebody knocked at the door. They used the little knocker – rat-a-tat-tat! Kim opened the door. He saw the two children looking down at him in delight and surprise.

"Hallo!" said the boy. "Do you really live here?"

"Yes," said Kim. "I hope you don't mind. It was empty when we found it, and there was nobody to say who it belonged to. Do *you* want to come and live here?"

The children laughed and laughed. "No, you funny little thing!" said the girl. "Of course we don't. We live in that big house up the garden."

"Oh, this isn't your house?" said Kim.

"It used to be our dog's kennel," said the boy with a giggle. "But we don't keep a dog now, so the kennel has been empty for a long time. Today we saw smoke at the bottom of the garden, and we came down to see what it was. And we suddenly saw a chimney on our dog's kennel, and two little windows, and a front door with a knocker!"

"We *did* get a surprise!" said the girl. "But oh, it's simply lovely! You have made the kennel into the prettiest little house I ever saw in my life!"

"So it was your dog's kennel!" said Mickle. "Oh, I do hope you won't want it for another dog."

"No, Mummy says dogs bark too much," said the boy. "So you're quite safe."

"May we really go on living here, then?" asked Kim, in delight.

"Of course," said the girl. "We'll never tell anyone about you, we promise. But please, please may we sometimes come down, knock at your door, and talk to you? You know, it's very exciting to have a brownie house at the bottom of our garden, with real brownies living there."

"You *are* nice," said Mickle. "Listen – we're having a party this afternoon. Would you like to come? You can't get inside the house comfortably, I'm afraid, but you could eat buns and biscuits out on the grass."

The two children squealed for joy. "Oh, *yes!*" said the girl. "Do, do let us come. We shall see all your friends then. And oh, little brownie, would you like me to lend you my best dolls' tea set for the party? It's very pretty, with a blue and yellow pattern."

"Thank you very much," said Mickle. "We haven't really got enough cups and plates, and we'd love to borrow yours."

So they borrowed the tea set, and it looked lovely in the little brownie house, set out on the round table. The party was simply lovely – but the two who enjoyed it most were the children, as you can guess. It was such a treat to sit and look at all the little folk coming to the dog's kennel, dressed in their best, knocking at the blue door, and saying "How do you do" to Mickle and Kim!

I won't tell you the names of the children, in case you know them – because they don't want anyone else to visit the brownie house and frighten away their tiny friends. But don't you think they're lucky to have a dog kennel that is used by Mickle and Kim?

41

The little pig squealed

There was once a toy pig in the playroom who had a most piercing squeal. "Eeeeeee!" he would squeal, "Eeeeeeeeee!"

At first the toys thought it was funny. Not one of them had a voice as loud as the pig's squeal. But they soon grew tired of the squeal.

"Now stop it," they said to the toy pig. "There's nothing whatever to squeal about. Nobody should squeal unless something is the matter."

"When can I squeal then?" asked the pig. "When can I go 'Eee, eee, eeeEEEE!' "

"*Don't*," said the teddy bear, putting his paws to his ears. "You can only

squeal when you are frightened of something, Pig. Then we'll come and rescue you."

"But don't squeal unless something *is* the matter!" said the toy mouse.

For two whole days the little pig didn't squeal. Nothing was the matter. Nothing frightened him. Well, there wasn't anything to be frightened of in the quiet playroom!

"My squeal will go if I don't use it," thought the little pig to himself. He tried it very softly. "Eeeeeeeeee. Oh, it's still there. It sounds funny if I squeal softly, though. I want to squeal loudly. But there's nothing the matter!"

Then he suddenly saw his own shadow behind him. He wasn't a bit frightened of it, but he pretended to be.

"Eeee, eee, EEEE!" he squealed, and all the toys jumped in fright.

"What is it, what is it?" cried the teddy bear, running over to the pig.

"Something dark and big is behind me," said the little pig.

"It's only your own shadow!" said the teddy bear, looking. "Silly little pig! Don't squeal at your own shadow again!"

The pig had enjoyed his squeal. He wanted to squeal again. It was fun to make the toys jump and come rushing over to him.

It began to rain the next day. The raindrops pattered on the window and the pig heard them. He knew quite well what they were but he thought he would squeal and pretend to be afraid. So he squealed.

"Eeeeeeee! Eeeeeeee!"

The little pig began to think it really was great fun to scare everyone when he squealed. He squealed for all kinds of things the next day!

"Eee-eee-EEEEEE! I'm sure I heard the cat outside the playroom door!"

And every single time all the toys came running over to him, scared to hear him squeal. They were very cross when they found there was really nothing the matter. They told him off.

"What did we tell you, Pig? You are not to squeal unless something *serious* is the matter! You are very naughty."

The toys went back to their game. They were playing with the bricks out of the brick box and building a lovely little house for one of the small dolls.

"If that silly, stupid little pig squeals again I shan't take any notice," said the teddy bear, building a nice little front door.

"Nor shall I," said the toy mouse, looking for a brick that would do for a chimney. "He just squeals to make us jump."

"Well, let him squeal," said a big skittle, who was looking on. "He'll soon get tired of it if none of us pays any attention."

Now up on the big bookcase was a pile of books. The children had put them there ready to lend to someone who was poorly. They hadn't piled them up very well, and every time a car went down the road, the bookcase shook and the pile of books slid nearer and nearer to the edge of the shelf.

At last a lorry came by, and the bookcase shook so much that the pile of books toppled over in a heap. Down they went, crash-crash-crash!

Nobody noticed that they had fallen on top of the little pig, who happened to be on the floor just below. They covered him up completely.

He tried to squeal, but he couldn't. He wriggled a little and moved one of the books. Then he could squeal.

How he squealed. You should have heard him! "EEEEEEEEEE!" It was almost as loud as a toy train's whistle. It made the toys jump.

"That pig again!" said the teddy bear. "Screaming for nothing as usual, I suppose."

"Well, let him," said the skittle, looking round. "I can't see him anywhere. He's probably in the toy cupboard, pretending he's been shut in, and he's squealing for us to rush over and let him out."

"Well, we won't," said the teddy bear. "There, look – I've put on two chimneys. Don't they look fine?"

"EEEEEEEEEEEE!" squealed the pig, under the pile of books.

"Squeal away," said the toy mouse. "We're tired of squeals that don't mean a thing. Now let me see – I think there are enough bricks left to build a wall."

"Eeeeeeee," squealed the pig, but now his squeal wasn't quite so loud. A big book was pressing down so hard on his middle that it was spoiling his squeal.

"There he goes again," said the teddy bear. "I'm surprised he doesn't get tired of it when he knows we're not going rushing to find him!"

"Eeee-eee," squealed the pig, still more faintly. "Eeee."

"Ah, he'll soon stop," said the skittle. "I wonder where he is. If he's in the toy cupboard you'd think he would rattle at the door."

"Eeeee," said the pig, and now his squeal was so faint that it could hardly be heard. The big book had broken it.

"You know – I really think we ought to look for the pig," said the mouse, suddenly. "I mean – he doesn't usually squeal so *softly*. Perhaps there *is* something wrong."

So they all went to look for him – and there he was, buried under the books, feeling very sorry for himself indeed. Not a bit of his squeal was left!

"He's here – under the books!" said the bear. The toys dragged the books away and the little pig stood up unsteadily on his legs. "I squealed," he said, in a faint voice. "I squealed for help – and you didn't come."

"I know," said the teddy bear. "But it was your own fault, Pig. You squealed for nothing so often that we didn't know when you really *were* squealing for something. Still, no harm's done, as far as I can see. You're safe and sound – no bones broken!"

"Yes, but my *squeal's* broken," said the pig, sadly. "That big book pressed on it so hard that in the end it broke. I can't squeal any more. I've tried."

He tried again – but no squeal came, only a curious little sigh. The toys stared at him.

"Well," said the bear, "I never *did* like your squeal, Pig – and as you used it for the wrong things, it really does serve you right to lose it."

"I think the same," said the mouse. "But I'm sorry for you, Pig. You can come and live in the brick house we've built till you feel better about things. That will be a little treat for you."

So now the pig is living in the little brick house till he feels better. He doesn't know if his squeal will come back again or not – but if it does he'll be careful how he uses it!

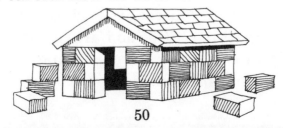

50

The little policeman

George had a lovely present on his eighth birthday. It was a policeman's uniform! It was small, just made to fit him, and the helmet was marvellous.

George was very proud of it. It came in a big box, and George took out the pieces of the uniform one by one. There was the coat with buttons down the front, the trousers, and a belt. There was the helmet, very grand indeed – and there was a notebook too, with a pencil tied to it with a piece of string!

"Just like our village policeman has!" said George to his mother. "When he came to our school the other day to tell our teacher that her dog was found, he brought out a black notebook just like this, with a pencil tied to it. I *shall* feel important dressed up like a policeman!"

When Saturday came, George thought he would be a policeman all day long. So he dressed up in his uniform. First he put on the trousers. Then he put on the coat. Then he buckled the belt round him and put the notebook and pencil into his pocket. And last of all he put on the helmet with the strap round his chin.

"Do I look smart?" he asked his mother.

"Simply marvellous," said his mother. "Just like a real policeman, George, only a bit smaller. Maybe you will catch a thief! Then you would really feel like a proper policeman." She smiled.

George went off to show himself to his friends. At first they didn't know it was George, and they stared in surprise to see such a small policeman walking along. George walked slowly just as the village policeman did, and the children all looked at him in amazement.

"Why, it's George!" cried Ann suddenly. "It's only George! But doesn't he look *real*!"

"Move on there, please, move on!" said George in a deep, gruff voice. The children squealed with laughter.

"Oh, you do look smart, George!" said Jane. "You really do!"

George thought he would go and show himself to his aunt, who lived in a farm over the fields. So he grinned at the children and then went off down the lane, walking slowly and grandly, feeling every inch a policeman.

But his aunt was out. That was most disappointing. George set off back home again.

"I wish I could meet someone, then I could pretend they are a thief or something," thought George to himself. "Oh – I know what I'll do! I'll hide in the hedge here and wait till somebody comes by. I'll pretend that I have to take notice of everything they wear and do. That will be fun! They won't see me. I can write it all down in my notebook as if I was a real policeman."

Just then a car drove up. It belonged to Farmer Straw. He jumped out, slammed his car door, and went through the field gate nearby to look at his crop of winter wheat.

George thought he wouldn't write down anything about him because he had disappeared so quickly. He watched the farmer going up the field to the next gate.

George twiddled his pencil and wished somebody else would come by. "I'd like them to come by slowly so that I could put down everything about them," thought George. "But people seem to walk along so quickly!"

He waited a minute or two, hidden well in the hedge. And then he saw somebody coming. Good!

It was a man. George began to write in his notebook: A man is coming by.

George looked up to see what the man was like. Then he wrote again: He is a tall dark man, and he has a little black moustache. He is wearing dark trousers and a torn raincoat, sort of brown-coloured.

The man came slowly by. George peered out of the hedge, thinking that he hadn't a very nice face. He noticed that the man had a scar down his left cheek.

"That might be important, if I was a real policeman taking notes," thought George. He wrote it down: There is a scar on his left cheek.

Just as the man came near to where George was hidden, he stopped. George thought that the man had seen him and was going to ask him why he was hiding, and his heart beat fast. He thought the man might be cross with him. But the man didn't even look into the hedge – he just looked up and down the lane, and then shaded his eyes to see Farmer Straw across the fields.

The man has a very old brown felt hat, wrote down George. His shoes are brown and one is split at the toe.

Then the man did such an extraordinary thing that George forgot to write any more. The man ran straight to Farmer Straw's car, opened the door, jumped in, set the engine going, and was away down the lane before George could say a word.

George stared at the disappearing car with his eyes and mouth wide open. Why had the man done that? Was he a friend of Farmer Straw's? How was Farmer Straw going to get home? It was very peculiar.

Then he heard the farmer shouting. Farmer Straw had seen and heard his car going away, and he was yelling in rage. He ran down to the field gate and looked down the lane. It was now empty. The man and the car were miles away!

George came suddenly out of the

hedge and made the farmer jump. He stared at the funny little policeman.

"Who in the world are you?" he asked in surprise.

"I'm George Hall," said George. "I'm not really a policeman. I got this uniform for my birthday."

"Well, it's a pity you *aren't* a real policeman!" said the farmer. "Then you might have been smart enough to catch the thief who has stolen my car!"

"Well, anyway, I know exactly what he's like," said George, opening his notebook.

The farmer laughed. "Oh no, you don't!" he said. "Children walk about with their eyes shut these days, it seems to me! They never notice anything!"

"Well, I've written down in my notebook everything I noticed about that man," said George. "See – here it is."

George read out aloud what he had written: "A man is coming by. He is a tall dark man and he has a little black moustache. He is wearing dark trousers and a torn raincoat, sort of brown-coloured. There is a scar on his left cheek. The man has a very old brown felt hat. His shoes are brown and one is split at the toe."

The farmer listened in the greatest astonishment. "My word! That's a perfectly splendid description of the man, I should think! He was too far away for me to see, of course – but if we give that description in at the police station I shouldn't think it would be very long before the thief is seen and caught!"

"You don't mean that you want to give my notebook in at the police station, do you?" cried George.

"Yes!" said the farmer, taking it from George. "You've acted like a real policeman, my boy, and I rather think you will be the means of the thief being caught. Come along!"

So down to the police station went the farmer and George, and very soon

George was telling the policeman there all that he had seen from his hiding-place in the hedge. The real policeman read George's notebook and then put down everything all over again in his own big notebook.

"This is very valuable," he said. "We can radio this information to all the police stations in the county, and every policeman can watch for a man with a little black moustache, and a scar on his left cheek, driving Farmer Straw's car. I expect he will alter the number plate, so it's not much use giving the number – but if you'll tell it to me, sir, I will add it to my notes . . ."

Very soon George's notes were being radioed to police miles away. George felt enormously proud. He marched back home with his head in the air, and told his mother all that had happened. She couldn't believe it.

"Oh no, George!" she said. "This is just a little tale of yours! Don't make up stories like that, dear."

But when the village policeman came knocking at the door that afternoon to tell her that the thief was caught, all because of George's notes, she *had* to believe it!

"The man changed the number-plate of the car," said the policeman. "But one of our men knew him to be the thief because of the scar on his left cheek. George had that down in his notes, you know. So he stopped the car and asked the man for his driving licence and he hadn't got it, of course! So now he has been caught, and we are very grateful indeed to George, because this man has stolen many cars before. He was caught about a hundred miles away from here, so he had gone a good distance already."

"Well done, George!" said his mother, and she hugged him. "I never thought you actually would act like a *real* policeman when I gave you your uniform. I *am* proud of you!"

George was proud too – but he was even prouder a week later when a little box arrived for him. Inside was a real policeman's whistle, with a note.

"For George, the little policeman, from Jim, the big policeman," said the note.

Wasn't that lovely for him? You should hear the whistle – it *would* make you jump!

The little steamroller man

T he little steamroller man was such a tiresome nuisance. His toy steamroller went by clockwork, and when it was wound up the steamroller man did all sorts of annoying things with it.

He would drive straight at the little toy farmyard and knock down the trees, the fences, and even chase the farm animals, too, if they didn't get out of his way.

He would drive right over the clockwork mouse's tail and make him squeal, and once he drove the steamroller over the teddy bear's paw when he was lying down asleep. The teddy bear was very angry indeed.

"Now, look here, Rollerman," he said. "The very next time you do a thing like that you won't be wound up when you run down. See? Then you'll have to stand your toy steamroller in the corner by itself, because you won't be able to make it go – unless you want to push it!"

"Rubbish!" said the little tin man, and didn't take a bit of notice. Next time the golden-haired doll wound him up he drove straight at a dear little house that had been built of bricks, and crash! Down it went!

"*Now* what will the children say tomorrow?" said the teddy bear, angrily. "They built that, as you very well know, Rollerman."

"That settles it," said the pink rabbit. "In future *no*body is to wind up the steamroller, nobody at all."

So nobody did, and the little rollerman was very cross. He thought he would try to wind up the roller himself. He hadn't ever done it before because he was afraid that the steamroller might start

64

off without him while he was winding it. But he put a big wooden brick in front of it, so that it couldn't go without him.

He kicked away the brick and leapt into the little cab of the steamroller just as it began to move. "Aha!" he shouted to the watching toys. "You thought you'd stopped me from driving my steamroller, but you haven't. I can wind it up myself, in future!"

And he did, too. He was more of a nuisance than ever. He drove his steamroller as fast as ever he could, and dear me, the things he did! He drove straight at the skittles standing up in a neat row – and biff, bang, thud, down they all went at once.

Then he drove at the toy soldiers when they were marching in a row with their captain at their head – and they had to run for their lives, which is not a nice thing for any kind of soldier to do. The little rollerman laughed so much that he almost fell off his steamroller.

The toys never knew when the

steamroller would come trundling over the floor at them. They couldn't sit down to have a talk without having to get out of its way. They couldn't set out tea on one of the little tables without having it all knocked over by the steamroller.

"What are we going to *do* about it?" said the pink rabbit, fiercely, when he had been bumped hard from behind by the steamroller and was almost knocked flying. "We've got to do *some*thing!"

They all looked at one another. It was all very well to say *some*thing had to be done – but what?

The clockwork mouse spoke up timidly. "Please, I've got an idea!"

"Speak up, then," said the teddy bear kindly. "You're a very small mouse so it must be a very small idea – but we'll certainly listen to it."

"Well," said the clockwork mouse, "you know how the steamroller man puts a brick in front when he winds up the steamroller – to keep it from running away before he can jump into the cab? My idea is this – couldn't I run at the brick with my sharp little nose and push it right away when the tin man is winding up the steamroller?"

"What good would that be?" asked the bear.

"Don't you see?" said the mouse. "The steamroller would run away all by itself – and if we managed to have it pointing to the open door it would run out into the passage and might never come back."

"Well – it's not a very bright idea, but it's worth trying," said the pink rabbit. "Look at the steamroller now – it's already pointing in the direction of the door. Bear, do you think you could help me to push the door wide open?"

The bear and the pink rabbit together pushed the door open. Then all the toys waited for the rollerman to wind up the steamroller for its next run.

He put the usual brick in front of it. Then he began to wind it up.

Urrrr-urrr-urrr-urrr! But before he had finished, up rushed the little clockwork mouse at top speed and bumped into the brick with his nose. It went flying off to the side, and before the rollerman could do anything about it, his steamroller had started off without him!

"Hey! Stop! Stop!" yelled the rollerman in fright. "Wait for me!"

But the steamroller didn't wait. It was wound up and it had to go, rolling its way over the carpet, flattening down all the little wrinkles.

The steamroller went rolling out of the door and into the passage. The little tin man went after it. The toys went to the door to watch.

"Good gracious! It's making for the stairs!" said the bear, suddenly. "Look! Oh, dear – it will fall headlong down them and be broken!"

Well, the toys hadn't meant *that* to happen, of course. The steamroller came to the top of the stairs just as the little man caught it up. He swung himself into the cab – but he couldn't stop it going down the stairs!

It fell down the first step, and turned upside down, and then rolled down to the next one. The little tin man shouted loudly. "Save us, save us!" But nobody could save them, of course. The steamroller bumped down every single stair to the bottom, turning upside down five times as it went. The tin man fell out. The clockwork mouse began to cry.

"Don't cry," said the pink rabbit. "It wasn't really your fault. Oh, dear – what a thing to happen! I suppose the steamroller is quite broken."

But it wasn't! One of the children found it and was most astonished to see it lying on its side at the bottom of the stairs. He found the tin man, too, and took them both to the playroom.

"*How* you managed to get out of this room and go all the way down the stairs by yourself is a real puzzle!" said the little boy, looking at his steamroller.

"You're not broken anywhere, either. Sit back in your cab, little rollerman, and cheer up – you'll be able to drive it again."

"Perhaps the little rollerman will have learnt his lesson," said the bear to the rabbit. "Perhaps he won't be tiresome any more. Perhaps he'll be kind and good."

Well, I'd like to tell you that he was – but alas, he wasn't! He glared down at all the toys from the cab of the little steamroller.

"I'll punish you for planning to knock away that brick!" he shouted.

"I'll teach you to do things like that to me! Look out for yourselves in future – I'll run you all down, I'll go over your tails and your toes, I'll knock over the whole farmyard, and I'll drive straight into the dolls' house and break the windows. As for that horrid little clockwork mouse, he'd better go and live with the real mice before I roll right into him!"

The toys ran away in fright. This was worse than ever. The tin man got down from his little cab and went to wind up his steamroller. The toys listened for the usual noise – urrrr-urr-urr-urr.

But it didn't come. They peeped out from the toy cupboard to see why. They saw the tin man standing by the steamroller, looking puzzled.

"Where's the key?" he said. "It's gone. It was fixed in so tightly, too – nobody could possibly have taken it out. *What's happened to it*?"

"Ah – it must have been knocked out when the steamroller fell downstairs!" said the bear, gleefully. "It's gone! You'll never be able to run into us again because you can't wind up your steamroller! Ha, ha, ha!"

"HURRAY!" yelled everyone. "It serves you right."

So it did. The tin man wondered and wondered where his key had gone. He even went to look for it. But it had been brushed up into a dust-pan and thrown away. Nobody ever saw it again.

So now the little rollerman can't drive his steamroller at all, and he's very miserable. Perhaps when he says he's sorry and tries to do something kind the toys will be friends with him – but it's really his own fault, isn't it?

The little sugar house

Mrs Biscuit kept a cake shop in Tweedle Village. All the boys and girls liked her shop because she had such exciting things in the window – gingerbread men, pastry cats and dogs, chocolate horses, and delicious iced cakes.

Mrs Biscuit would have been a very nice woman if only she hadn't told so many stories. She really didn't seem to know *how* to tell the truth.

"Was this cake baked today?" a customer would ask. "Is it quite fresh?"

"Oh yes, madam, it's just new," Mrs Biscuit would answer, knowing quite well that the cake was stale and dry.

Mrs Biscuit was mean, too. She never gave anything away if she could help it, not even broken bits of stale cake. She made those into puddings for herself.

Now one day she thought she would make a very fine iced cake and put it into the middle of her window to make people stare.

"If they come and look at my iced cake they will see my buns, my biscuits, and other things," thought Mrs Biscuit, "and perhaps they will buy them."

So she made a beautiful iced cake with pink roses all round the edge. But she didn't know what to put in the middle.

"I think I'll make a little sugar house," she said to herself. "It shall have windows and a door and two chimneys. Everyone will be delighted to see it."

So she made a wonderful little house all out of sugar. She gave it two red chimneys, four windows, and a little brown door made of chocolate. She put pink sugar roses on the walls, and when it had set hard she popped it on the very top of her big cake. Then she put it into the window.

At first everyone came to look at it – but after a little while they thought it was boring.

"Why don't you put someone into your house?" asked a little girl. "Houses are meant to be lived in, aren't they, even sugar houses? Why don't you go to the Very-Little-Goblins and ask one to live in your sugar house? Then people would come every day to see him opening the chocolate door and looking out of the sugar windows at the pink roses."

Well, Mrs Biscuit thought that was a very good idea. She put on her bonnet and went to where the Very-Little-Goblins lived in their mushroom houses.

"Would one of you like to come and live in a sugar house with pink roses on the walls?" she asked. "It's not like your mushroom houses, up one night and gone the next, so that you have to keep on moving. It stays on my big iced cake for weeks and weeks, and is very beautiful indeed."

The Very-Little-Goblins came out of their mushroom houses and stared at her.

"We have heard that you tell stories," said their chief goblin. "We are very truthful people, you know, and we couldn't live with anyone who didn't tell the truth."

"Of course I tell the truth!" said Mrs Biscuit crossly. "Why, I've never told a story in my life!"

"Well, that's splendid," said the chief goblin, quite believing her. "I shall be very pleased to let my eldest son come and live in your little sugar house tomorrow."

"Thank you," said Mrs Biscuit, delighted, and she went home.

Soon everyone knew that one of the Very-Little-Goblins was coming to live on the big iced cake in the window, and all the children of Tweedle Village were tremendously excited.

The next day Twinkle, the Very-Little-Goblin, arrived at Mrs Biscuit's shop. She lifted him up on to the iced cake in the window and showed him the sugar house. He was simply delighted with it.

He opened the little chocolate door and went inside. He had brought no furniture with him, so he asked Mrs Biscuit if she would make him a little chocolate bed, two sugar chairs, and a chocolate table. He said he would put up curtains at the windows and buy a little carpet for the floor.

Soon the sugar house was quite ready for him, and all the children of the village came to peep at it. It was most exciting to see the goblin open the door and shake his little mats. It was lovely to see him draw the curtains and lean out of the window. Sometimes he would carry his chocolate table and one of his sugar chairs on to the big sugary space outside the little house, and have his dinner there.

Mrs Biscuit did such a lot of trade. A great many people came into the shop to see the iced cake with its sugar house, and of course they had to buy something, so Mrs Biscuit began to be quite rich.

For a little while she remembered to tell the truth to people – and then she forgot.

"Is this chocolate cake fresh?" asked Dame Tippy one morning.

"Oh yes, quite!" said Mrs Biscuit untruthfully, for the cake had been baked more than a week ago.

"Oh, you story-teller!" cried a tiny voice, and the Very-Little-Goblin peeped out of the sugar house. "You baked that last week."

"Dear, dear, so I did!" said Mrs Biscuit crossly, very angry to hear the goblin's voice. "Take this one instead, Dame Tippy."

The next day a little girl came in for thirty pence worth of fresh buns. Mrs Biscuit quickly took six stale ones from a tray at the back of the shop and popped them into a bag.

"These are nice and new," she said to the little girl.

"You naughty story-teller! They're as hard as bricks!" cried the little goblin, poking his head out of the window of the sugar house.

"You be quiet! These buns were only baked this morning," said Mrs Biscuit angrily.

"Oooh, the story-teller! Oh, little girl, don't give her your money. She's telling you stories!"

The little girl ran out of the shop with her money in her hand, but Mrs Biscuit called her back.

"I'm only joking with you," she said to the child. "See, here are some lovely new buns I baked early this morning."

"Yes, take those," cried the goblin. "They're all right."

When the little girl had gone, Mrs Biscuit turned to grumble at the goblin. To her surprise he was rolling up his carpet and taking down his curtains.

"What are you doing?" she asked.

"Going home," answered the goblin. "You don't suppose I'm going to stay here with a nasty old woman who tells stories, do you? We Very-Little-Goblins hate that!"

"Oh, don't go," begged Mrs Biscuit. "Don't go! Everyone will wonder why you've gone."

"Oh no, they won't, because I shall tell them," said the goblin, tying up his carpet into a roll.

"Please, please, Goblin, stay with me. I'll make you a beautiful little garden seat out of chocolate and ginger if you'll stay," begged Mrs Biscuit. "And I won't tell stories any more, I promise."

"Well, if you do, I'll tell people the truth," said the goblin, unrolling his carpet again. "So you be careful, Mrs Biscuit."

Mrs Biscuit was very careful for a few days and the goblin didn't speak a word. Then one morning, a poor beggar-woman came in and asked Mrs Biscuit for a stale cake.

"A stale cake? Why, I haven't such a thing in the place!" cried Mrs Biscuit. "Be off with you!"

"Oh, you mean old woman!" cried the goblin's tiny voice, and he flung open his chocolate front door. "Where are those cakes you baked last Thursday that haven't been sold yet?"

"I've eaten them myself," said Mrs Biscuit in a rage. "Mind your own business!"

"You're a story-teller," said the goblin. "There they are up on that shelf. You give them to the poor beggar-woman this very minute, or I'll go back to Mushroom Town."

Mrs Biscuit dragged the cakes down, put them into a bag and threw them across the counter. The beggar-woman thanked her and went off with them.

Mrs Biscuit didn't care to say anything to the goblin, but she was very angry. He went into his sugar house and slammed the door. He was angry too, to think that anyone could be so mean.

That afternoon a thin little boy crept into the shop and asked for a stale crust. He was dreadfully hungry, and Mrs Biscuit stared at him crossly. Another beggar!

She was just going to say that she had no stale crusts when she saw the goblin peeping at her out of one of the windows of his sugar house. She hurriedly took down half a stale loaf and gave it to the little boy.

He was so grateful that he took her plump hand and kissed it. It was the first time that Mrs Biscuit had been kissed for years, and dear me, she *did* like it! She suddenly smiled at the little boy, and felt sorry to see how thin he was. And then she took down a fine new chocolate cake, and gave it to him.

"Oh!" he said in delight. "You kind woman! Is that really for me?"

He went out of the shop singing. Mrs Biscuit looked at the place on her hand where the little boy had kissed it, and a nice warm feeling crept into her heart. It was really rather pleasant to be kind, she thought. She would try it again.

She looked up and saw a crowd of people looking in at her window. And she saw that the goblin was doing a strange, light-hearted little dance round and round the top of the cake, making all the passers-by stare in surprise.

"What are you doing that for?" she asked in astonishment.

"Oh, I'm so pleased to see you do a kind act that I've got to dance!" said the tiny goblin. Everyone watched him, and soon quite a dozen people came in to buy cakes. Mrs Biscuit did a good morning's trade.

The next time someone came begging,

Mrs Biscuit decided to be kind and generous again, to get the nice warm feeling in her heart. So she packed up a cherry pie in a box and put some ginger buns in a bag for the old man who came asking for a crust. He was so surprised and delighted that he could hardly say thank you. The little goblin threw open his door and began to sing a loud song all about Mrs Biscuit's kindness, and soon half the village came to hear it. Mrs Biscuit blushed red, and didn't know where to look.

Then Mr Straw, the farmer, came to buy a big ginger cake for his wife's birthday. Now, there were two ginger cakes in the shop, one baked a good time back and one baked that very morning. Mrs Biscuit took up the stale one and popped it into a bag.

"You're sure that's fresh, now?" said Farmer Straw. Mrs Biscuit opened her mouth to say untruthfully that it was, when she stopped.

No, that would be a mean unkind

thing to say, especially when the cake was for Mrs Straw's birthday.

"Er – well, no, this one isn't very fresh," she said. "I'll give you a fresher one, only baked this morning."

The little goblin, who was peeping out of his window, ready to cry out that she was a story-teller, gave a shout of delight.

"She's a truthful old dame!" he cried. "She's a kind old woman!"

"Dear me," said Mr Straw, looking round. "That's your little goblin, isn't it? Well, it's nice of you to let me have the fresh cake, Mrs Biscuit, when you've got one that is not quite so fresh. I'm much obliged to you. Perhaps you'll be good enough to come to my wife's birthday party this afternoon?"

"I'd be very pleased to," said Mrs Biscuit, thankful that she hadn't given him the stale cake – for how dreadful it would have been to go to a birthday party and see everyone eating a stale cake she had sold as fresh!

Well, that was the last time Mrs Biscuit ever thought of telling a story or being mean. She felt so nice when she had told the truth or been kind to someone that she soon found she simply couldn't tell a story or be unkind any more. And in a short time people liked her so much that they always bought their cakes and pies from her, and she became rich enough to buy a little cottage and go there to live.

She took the iced cake with her, with the little sugar house on top. She put it on a table in the front window to remind her of the days when she had kept a cake shop – and would you believe it? – that Very-Little-Goblin is still there, shaking his carpet every day and opening his windows to let in the sunshine!

That shows she is still a truthful, kind old dame, and if you ever pass her cottage and see the iced cake in the window, with the little sugar house on top, don't be afraid of knocking at her door and asking if you may see the Very-Little-Goblin. Mrs Biscuit will be delighted to show you round.

The little toymaker

George and Fanny were excited because Mummy had said they could go out for a picnic by themselves.

"If you cross over the road very carefully and go to the hill above the long field you should be all right," said Mummy.

So they set off, with George carrying the basket. In the basket were some egg sandwiches, two rosy apples, a small bar of chocolate, and two pieces of ginger cake. There was a bottle of lemonade as well, and George and Fanny kept thinking of the cool lemonade as they crossed the road, went through the long field and up the hill. They did feel so very thirsty!

There were ash and sycamore trees up on the hill. Already they were throwing down their seeds on the wind – ash spinners that spun in the breeze, and sycamore keys that twirled down to the ground.

George picked some up and looked at them. "Aren't they nice?" he said. "Throw some up into the air, Fanny, and see them spin in the wind to the ground. The tree is pleased to see them twirling in the wind, because then it knows that its seeds are travelling far away to grow into big new trees."

After a while the children sat down to have their lunch. They began on the egg sandwiches, but before they had taken more than a few bites they saw a most surprising sight. A very small man, not much higher than George's teddy bear at home, came walking out from behind a gorse bush. He carried two baskets with him. One was empty and one was full. The full one had sandwiches and milk in it, and the children thought that the small man must be having a picnic, just as they were.

The little man didn't see them. He had a very long white beard that he had tied neatly round his waist to keep out of the way of his feet. He wore enormous glasses on his big nose, and he had funny pointed ears and a hat that had tiny bells on. The bells tinkled as he walked. Fanny wished and wished she had a hat like that.

"What a very little man!" said Fanny. "Do you suppose he is a pixie or a brownie?"

"*Ssh!*" said George. "Don't talk. Let's watch."

So they watched. The little man walked along, humming a song – and suddenly he tripped over a root, and down he went! His full basket tipped up, and out fell his sandwiches and milk. The bottle broke. The sandwiches split open and fell into bits on the grass.

"Oh, what a pity!" cried George, and he ran at once to help.

The little man was surprised to see
him. George picked him up, brushed the
grass off his clothes, and looked sadly at
the milk and sandwiches.

"Your picnic is no use," he said. "Come
and share ours. Do!"

The small man smiled and his face
lit up. He picked up his baskets and
went to where the children had spread
their picnic food. Soon he was sitting
down chatting to them, sharing their
sandwiches, cake, and chocolate. He
was very pleased.

"Why was one of your baskets
empty?" asked Fanny. "What were you
going to put into it?"

"Ash and sycamore keys," said the
small man. "There are plenty on this
hill."

"Shall we help you to fill your
basket?" said George. "We've eaten
everything now, and Fanny and I would
like to help you."

"Oh, please do," said the small man.
So the three of them picked up the

ash and sycamore keys, and put them neatly into the basket.

"Why do you collect these?" asked Fanny. "I would so like to know. Do you burn them or something?"

"Oh, no. I'm a toymaker and I use them for keys for my clockwork toys," said the little man. "Come home with me, if you like. I'll show you."

He took them over the top of the hill and there, under a mossy curtain, was a tiny green door set in the side of the hill. The little man pushed a sycamore key into the door and unlocked it. Inside was a tiny room, set with small furniture and a big work table.

And on the table were all kinds of toys! They were made out of hazelnut shells, acorns, chestnuts, pine cones, and all sorts of things! The small man had cleverly made bodies and heads and legs and wings, and there were the toys, very small, but very quaint and beautiful. The children stared at them in delight.

"Now, you see," said the little man, emptying out his basket of keys on to his work table. "Now, you see, all I need to do is to find keys to fit these toys, and then they can be wound up, and they will walk and run and dance. Just fit a few keys into the holes and see if you can wind up any of the toys."

In great excitement the two children fitted ash and sycamore keys into the toys, and George found one that fitted a pine-cone bird perfectly. He wound it up – and the bird danced and hopped, pecked and even flapped its funny wings. It was lovely to watch.

Soon all the toys were dancing about on the table, and the children clapped their hands. It was the funniest sight they had ever seen! They only had to fit a key to any of the toys, wind it up – and lo and behold, that toy came to life!

"I wish we hadn't got to go, but we must," said George at last. "Goodbye, little toymaker. I do love your toys."

"Choose one each!" said the little man.

So they did. Fanny chose the bird, and George chose a hedgehog made very cleverly out of a prickly chestnut-case and a piece of beech-mast. It ran, just like a real hedgehog does, when George wound it up.

And now those two toys are on their playroom mantelpiece at home, and they are so funny to watch when George and Fanny wind them up with ash and sycamore keys. I can't show you the toys – but you can go and find ash and sycamore keys in the autumn for yourself, if you like. There are plenty under the trees, spinning in the wind. Find a few, and see what good little keys they make for winding up fairy toys!

The rough little boy

Anna was to go to tea with her Auntie Susan. She loved her aunt, and was very pleased to be going all alone down the street to see her.

"I shall take her the beautiful bead necklace I was making for her yesterday," said Anna happily. "She will like that. And, Mummy, can I wear my lovely new red hair-ribbon?"

"Yes, you can," said Mummy, and she got the ribbon out of the box. She brushed Anna's hair, and tied the new red ribbon on one side. It did look nice. "I shall carry the bead necklace in my hand," said Anna. "Then I can look at it. It is so pretty. There are beads of all colours, Mummy – red, blue, green, yellow, brown and white. Do you think Auntie Susan will like it?"

"She will love it," said Mummy. "Now be careful to keep on the path, Anna, and don't go into the road at all. You don't need a hat. Run along now and come home again at six o'clock."

So off Anna went. She felt very proud of the red ribbon in her hair and very proud of the bead necklace in her hand. It had taken her a long time to thread. The beads were nice and big, made of coloured glass, and they shone brightly in the sun.

Just round the corner Anna saw a boy she didn't like a bit! It was Thomas, and he was rough. He was the kind of boy who loved to pull little girls' hair, and to snatch off little boys' caps. I expect you know the kind of boy. Nobody likes them much.

Well, there came Thomas, whistling loudly and looking for mischief. And as soon as he saw Anna he grinned. Ah, here was a little girl to tease!

He ran up to her. "What have you got in your hand?" he asked.

"Never mind," said Anna, and she put her hand behind her.

"Let me see," said Thomas, and he tried to open her hand. He hurt Anna, and the little girl had to open her fingers. The necklace fell to the pavement, the string broke, and the lovely beads rolled all over the place!

"You horrid, horrid boy!" cried Anna, with tears in her eyes. "I made that for my Auntie Susan. Help me to pick up the beads."

She bent down to pick them up – and Thomas caught sight of the new red ribbon. He snatched at it – and it came off. Then away went Thomas with the ribbon flying in his fingers, calling, "Here goes your red ribbon! Here goes your red ribbon!"

Anna didn't know whether to run after her ribbon or pick up her beads. She stood there with tears rolling down her cheeks. The horrid rude boy! He had

got her ribbon and broken her necklace.
"Here goes your red ribbon!" cried
Thomas, and he flapped it at Anna
down the road as he ran. He didn't
look where he was going and he ran
straight into a lamp-post. Down he went
and banged his head hard against the
post. How he yelled and cried!

102

Anna ran to help him. She pulled Thomas to his feet and wiped his hands clean. She looked at his hurt knee and tied it up with her handkerchief. He looked very red and ashamed when she had finished.

"Thank you," he said. "How funny of you to help somebody who teased you!"

"I still think you are a horrid little boy," said Anna, "but we have to help even horrid people if they are in trouble. You'd better go home to your mother. But give me back my red ribbon first."

"It's gone," said Thomas, looking all round for it. "Quite gone. The wind must have blown it away. I say – I'm really sorry."

"Well, you might help me to pick up my beads," said Anna, who meant to make Thomas do something. "I am very, very sad about my new ribbon. I'm going to tea with my Auntie, and she will think I'm most untidy without a ribbon in my hair."

Thomas went back down the street to

pick up the beads. He got a handful of them and then looked at Anna.

"Have you got a pocket to put them in?" he asked.

"No," said Anna. "I even have to keep my hanky up my sleeve. Oh dear! How shall I carry the beads?"

"I live just here," said Thomas, going into a nearby gate. "Come in and I'll see if I've got a box to put the beads in for you."

Anna went inside the gate and waited for Thomas. Presently he came out carrying an old chocolate box. It was very pretty indeed, and had a picture of a kitten on the front and a big piece of blue ribbon round the lid.

"Here you are," said Thomas, opening the box. "You can have this box. It's my best chocolate box, and I kept my marbles in it. But you can have it for helping me. Truly I am sorry I broke your necklace."

"Oh, thank you," said Anna, and she put all her beads into the chocolate box.

They made a nice rattly sound. "Well, I really don't mind about the necklace now, because I have this lovely box – and I can easily thread all the beads again. But it's a shame about my ribbon. I do hate going out to tea without a ribbon in my hair."

"I say! What about taking the ribbon off the chocolate box lid!" cried Thomas, pointing to the broad blue ribbon that went round the lid. He pulled it off and held it up. It was a fine piece, wide and silky and blue. "It's just right for you," said Thomas. "Your eyes are blue and the ribbon is blue! Can you tie it on?"

"I think so," said Anna. She put down her chocolate box and took the ribbon. She tied it neatly on her hair in a big bow. It did look nice.

"Anna, it's *much* prettier than the red ribbon!" said Thomas. And so it was. Anna looked lovely with it on her hair. She felt very pleased.

"Well, goodbye, Thomas," she said. "You may be a horrid, rough little boy, but you're quite nice and kind, too. I like that part of you."

"Will you come and play with me tomorrow?" asked Thomas. "I promise I won't be rough. You can keep my chocolate box for your very own."

"I'll ask my mother if I can come and play," said Anna. "Goodbye! What a lot I shall have to tell my Auntie Susan!"

And off she went with the blue ribbon in her hair and the chocolate box under her arm, the beads rattling gaily.

"Well, what a good thing I was kind to Thomas when he fell down," thought Anna. "I would never, never have known that he was anything but a very horrid, rough little boy. I think I *will* go and play with him tomorrow if Mummy says yes. And I might even give him my tiny blue car – if he isn't rough again!"

Well, Thomas has got the blue car – so he couldn't have been rough. It was a good thing for him that he met a kind child like Anna, wasn't it?

Tiptap's little trick

Mr Twisty went to market every Friday with two big baskets of goods to sell. In one basket he took vegetables or fruit, and in the other he took eggs.

"Old Twisty helps himself to other people's fruit and vegetables and eggs at night," said the people of the village. "He comes in the dark, like a shadow – and pulls up our lettuces and picks our peas and our fruit. He goes into our hen-houses and takes the eggs, as sly as a rat in the night!"

But nobody could catch old Twisty at it, nobody at all. He was as full of tricks and wily ways as a weasel.

"We'll have to play a trick on *him*,"

said Dame Ho-Ho at last. "So let's think hard."

They thought and they thought. Mr Flap frowned and Mr Flop scowled, they thought so hard. Mother Run-Round and old Mrs Scatter did their best to think of a way to trick Twisty and pay him back for his mean ways.

It was little Tiptap who thought of an idea. He told the others, and they laughed. "It's a bit silly," said Dame Ho-Ho, "but it *might* catch him."

"It's good," said Mr Flap. "We'll try it."

So the next day, when everyone was going to market, little Tiptap went, too. He had some strong rope coiled round his waist, and he laughed as he went.

He ran round a corner, tied the end of the rope to something there, and then came back again, holding his end. He waited till he saw Mr Twisty coming along with two heavy baskets.

Then Tiptap began to tug and pull at the rope for all he was worth. "Come up,

there!" he yelled. "Come along, will you!
Why won't you come? You'll be late for
market and I won't be able to sell you.
Come on, there!"

Mr Twisty stopped, put down his
baskets and watched. He liked seeing
people in difficulties.

Tiptap tugged and tugged at the rope
which was stretched as tight as could
be. "Come along, I tell you!" he cried.
"Acting like this on market day!"

"Ha-ha!" laughed Mr Twisty. "Ho-ho!
Your pig – or your cow or whatever it is
– wants to go a different way from you.
Ho-ho! He'll pull *you* round the corner
soon!"

Everyone was watching Tiptap.
Dame Ho-Ho was there, smiling.
Mr Flap and Mr Flop stood there,
nodding in delight. Mother Run-Round
and Mrs Scatter laughed loudly.

"All of you laughing at me and not
giving a hand to help!" cried Tiptap,
pulling hard. "Help, somebody!"

Mother Run-Round came up to help.

She tugged and pulled, too, but it wasn't any good. No animal came round the corner on the end of the rope.

"*Will* you come along?" shouted Tiptap, in a very angry voice. "I tell you, if you don't come I'll sell you for five pounds, here and now! I'm tired of you!"

Twisty pricked up his ears. What! Tiptap was so angry that he would sell this animal cheaply? Well, perhaps Twisty could get a good bargain.

"Here – I'll pull it round for you," he said. "And, if you like, I'll buy the creature. It will save you going to the market. But a stubborn, bad-tempered animal like this won't be worth much."

"You're right," said Tiptap, tugging. "If it's going to act like this at every corner I'll never get to market. You can have it for five pounds."

"Say three," said Twisty, and he took the rope-end from Tiptap. He pulled. My word – what animal could there be at the end of this rope? He couldn't budge

it! It must at least be a cow – or even a horse or donkey! He tugged and tugged. Yes – it must be a horse.

"Say four pounds," said Tiptap, "and your two baskets of goods. You won't want to carry those to market if you've got something else to tug along."

"A horse for four pounds!" thought Twisty in delight, still pulling hard. He turned to Tiptap.

"All right. Feel in my pocket and take four pounds. You can have the baskets, too."

"Thanks!" said Tiptap, and winked at everyone in delight. He picked up the baskets and looked into them. "Ah – these eggs must be yours, Mr Flap and Mr Flop. And these lettuces must belong to you, Mother Run-Round. They are just like you grow. And these . . ."

"You stop talking like that!" yelled Mr Twisty, in a rage. But he couldn't run after Tiptap because he didn't dare to leave go of the rope!

Tiptap and the others went off giggling. Mr Twisty nearly went mad trying to pull the rope hard enough to pull the animal to him.

Suddenly someone appeared at the corner. It was Mr Letters, the postman. He shouted at Mr Twisty.

"Hey, you! What do you think you're doing? You've nearly pulled the letter-box down. Is this a joke, or what?"

Mr Twisty stared at him. He ran quickly to the corner and looked round it. My, oh my – that rope was tied firmly round a stout red letter-box – and it was almost bent in half with Twisty's pulling! He gaped at it.

"B-b-b-but there should be a horse, or a cow or a pig, on the end of the rope," stammered Mr Twisty in dismay.

"Well, it must have turned into a letter-box, then," said Mr Letters. "And I'm afraid I must ask you to come to the police-station with me, Mr Twisty, on a charge of doing malicious damage to a public letter-box! That's for posting letters in, not for pulling down!"

Mr Twisty didn't wait a moment. He fled at top speed, caught the first bus he saw, and went to the Village of Far-Away. What with animals that turned into letter-boxes – and postmen that wanted to take him away – and everyone laughing at him – he just couldn't stay another moment.

The folk of the village saw him going by at top speed to catch the bus. How they laughed!

Tiptap divided the four pounds between everyone who had goods stolen from them by Twisty. And what do you think they did with it? They put it together again and gave a party for Tiptap!

"You got rid of mean old Twisty," they said. "You deserve a party, Tiptap. He'll never dare to come back again."

They were right. He never did.

Lazy little Pimmy

Pimmy was the pixie who lived in Pimmy Cottage at the end of Snapdragon Village. You could tell he was lazy because his garden was full of weeds, his windows were dirty, and his gate hung crooked.

Now one day it was very, very windy. Pimmy put on his red hat with the feather in it and went out. It was a silly hat to wear on a windy day, but Pimmy liked it very much. It was his best hat, and the feather made him feel grand.

The wind saw Pimmy's hat in delight. *Whooooo!* Just the kind of hat the wind liked to play with. It swept down on Pimmy, swished off his hat, and made it sail high in the air.

"Oh – bother, bother, bother!" cried Pimmy, as he saw his lovely hat whirled away. "Come back hat!"

But the hat didn't. It was enjoying itself. It sailed off, went over a tree, and then came down on the top of the shed in Dame Stern's garden.

"That's a nuisance," said Pimmy, screwing up his nose. "I daren't go and get my hat off Dame Stern's shed without asking her – and she may snap my head off, she's so bad-tempered."

Anyway, he went to ask if he might get it, because he really couldn't bear to lose such a lovely hat. He knocked on Dame Stern's door.

"If it's the washing, leave it on the step!" called a voice.

"It isn't," said Pimmy.

"Well, if it's the paper boy, bring me the right paper tomorrow, or I'll chase you all the way down the street and back again," said the voice.

Pimmy felt glad he wasn't the paper boy.

"It isn't the paper boy," he said. "It's Pimmy. My hat has been blown on top of your shed, Dame Stern, and please may I get it?"

"No, you may not," said Dame Stern. "You'll fall off and break your neck."

"I could climb up a ladder all right," said Pimmy politely.

"I haven't got a ladder," said Dame Stern. "But Old Man Stamper has. You might be able to borrow his."

Pimmy went off to Old Man Stamper's house. The old fellow was in his garden, digging.

"Please, Mister Stamper, could you lend me your ladder?" said Pimmy. "My hat's blown on to the top of Dame Stern's shed."

"What a silly hat to have," said Old Man Stamper. "Well – I'll lend you my ladder, but you must do something for me first. You run along to Mother Grumble's and ask her to let me have a little of her cough medicine. My cough's so bad at night."

118

Pimmy didn't want to go to Mother Grumble's. It was a long way to go, and he was afraid of her. But still, he wouldn't get the ladder if he didn't, and if he didn't get the ladder, he'd lose his hat. So he had to go.

He came to Mother Grumble's and knocked at the door. He could hear the old lady grumbling away to someone.

"And if it isn't one thing, it's another. One of my hens got loose this morning, and it pecked up all my lettuce, and then a stray dog came and dug up my carrot bed, and . . ."

Pimmy knocked again.

"And now here's someone come to the door, just as I've got settled down to have a cup of tea! Really, if it isn't one thing, it's another. Who's at the door? Speak up!"

"Pimmy the Pixie!" called Pimmy. "Please will you lend Old Man Stamper some of your cough medicine?"

"Well, if he isn't asking all day long for something or other!" said Mother

119

Grumble. "First it's a pinch of tea, then it's a box of matches, and now it's cough medicine. I haven't got a bottle to put some in for him. You'd better go and ask the chemist to let you have one, Pimmy. Then I'll give you some."

Pimmy groaned. The chemist lived over the other side of the hill. He set off again and came to the chemist.

"Hello, lazy little Pimmy," said the chemist, who had once had Pimmy for an errand boy and sent him away because he was so lazy. "What do *you* want?"

"Could you let me have an old medicine bottle for Mother Grumble?" said Pimmy.

"Ah, you want something for nothing, do you?" said the chemist. "No, no — if you want a bottle, you must do something to get it, Pimmy. I don't give something for nothing!"

"Well, what shall I do?" said Pimmy, feeling that he would never get home that day.

"See this parcel?" said the chemist. "Well, you take it to Mrs Flap's for me, and when you come back you shall have the bottle. See?"

Pimmy set off. Mrs Flap's house was half a mile away. Pimmy wished he had had his shoes mended the week before, as he should have done. There was a hole in one, and the stones kept coming in and hurting his foot.

He came to Mrs Flap's. Nobody answered the door. Pimmy knocked and knocked, more and more loudly. Then the window of the next house flew up, and an angry face looked out.

"What's all this noise? It sounds like a thousand postmen at the door – *knock*, *knock*, *knock*! Mrs Flap's not in. She's out shopping."

"Oh, dear," said Pimmy, looking at the angry face of Mr Glum. "I've come so far to bring her a parcel from the chemist."

"Well, I'll take it in for you if you'll do

something for me," said Mr Glum. "My dog hasn't been for his walk today, and he's longing for it. My leg's bad, and I can't take him. You just take him round the streets and back again, and when you come back I'll take the parcel in for Mrs Flap. Then you won't need to sit on her doorstep and wait."

"I don't like taking dogs for walks," said Pimmy. "And besides, I'm tired."

Mr Glum looked at him hard. "Ah, you're lazy little Pimmy, aren't you?" he said. "*You* wouldn't take a dog for a walk, no matter how hard he begged you, would you? You're too lazy."

He slammed down his window. Pimmy stared at it in despair. Mrs Flap might be hours before she came back from her shopping. He couldn't wait all that time. He would have to take Mr Glum's dog for a walk, even though his legs felt dreadfully tired.

So he shouted out loudly: "Mr Glum, Mr Glum, I'll take your dog out!"

The front door opened. Mr Glum

limped out with a very large dog on a lead. "Here you are," he said. "Take him for a nice run and come back again."

Pimmy took the lead and set off. He meant to go round the corner and sit down for ten minutes, and then take the dog home again. But the dog had other ideas.

Pimmy didn't take that dog for a run – it took Pimmy for a gallop. It was a large dog and a strong dog, and a very determined dog. It tore off down the street, and Pimmy was dragged after it.

"Here! Hi! Whoa!" panted Pimmy. But the dog took not the slightest notice. It rushed on like an express train, and Pimmy had to follow it. He ran and he ran, and he panted and he puffed. He had never in his life run so fast.

Then the dog suddenly turned and ran back to sniff an exciting smell. The lead wound itself round Pimmy's legs, and he sat down very suddenly. The dog

looked surprised and sniffed at Pimmy's ear.

"Don't, you horrid dog," panted Pimmy. "What do you mean by rushing off at top speed like that? Don't sniff in my ear – it tickles."

The dog sniffed at Pimmy's nose. Pimmy got up, and the dog at once started off at top speed again. But, luckily, this time it made for home. Pimmy tore along behind it, almost falling over his own feet.

He got back to Mr Glum's, his face hot and red, his breath coming in such loud pants that Mr Glum heard him before he even saw him. Mr Glum smiled one of his rare smiles.

"I see Scamper has been giving you a good run," he said. "Well, it will do you good, lazy little Pimmy. Here, here, Scamper! Come in. Where is the parcel you wanted me to give to Mrs Flap? Ah, there she is. You can give it to her yourself now."

He shut his door; Pimmy glared at it.

So he had taken that dreadful dog out for nothing! He scowled, gave the parcel to Mrs Flap, and set off wearily to the chemist's.

"What a long time you've been!" said the chemist. "Lazy as usual, I suppose – just crawled along, didn't you?"

"I've been rushing along at about sixty miles an hour!" said Pimmy, crossly, and he took the bottle the chemist held out to him. "Thank you. If I'd known how many miles I'd have had to run when I took that parcel for you, I wouldn't have done it!"

Pimmy took the bottle to Mother Grumble. She got up to fill it, grumbling away as usual. "If it isn't one thing, it's another. No sooner do I sit myself down than up I have to get again for lazy little fellows like you, Pimmy!"

Pimmy took the bottle of cough medicine to Old Man Stamper. The old man was very glad to have it. He took a dose at once.

"Could I borrow your ladder, please?"

said Pimmy. "You said I could if I brought you some cough medicine."

"Dear me, I'd forgotten," said Old Man Stamper. "There it is, look. Mind you bring it back."

Pimmy took the ladder. It was heavy. He staggered back to Dame Stern's garden.

"Oh, you've got the ladder, have you?" said Dame Stern. "Now you be careful not to tread on any of my beds, Pimmy!"

Pimmy was very careful. His arms ached with the heavy ladder and he was glad to put it up against the shed. He went up. Now at last, at last, he would get his lovely hat!

But it wasn't there! It was gone! Pimmy burst into tears. Dame Stern was surprised.

"What's the matter?" she called. "Oh, of course, your hat is gone. Yes, I saw it go. The wind came down and swept it away. I don't know where it went to."

Pimmy cried bitterly. He carried the heavy ladder back to Old Man Stamper.

Then he went home, still crying. And when he got there, what did he see in his very own garden but his lovely hat, feather and all!

"Oh – who brought you back?" he cried in delight, and put it on. The wind swept round him and shouted in his ear.

"I brought it back here, Pimmy. I was just playing a trick on you, that's all. I brought it back!"

"Oh, you mean, unkind wind!" cried Pimmy. "I've borrowed a heavy ladder and carried it ever so far – I've fetched cough medicine – I've carried a parcel – and I've taken a dog out for a run – all to get my hat, and now it's here! I'm tired out!"

"Do you good, do you good, lazy little Pimmy!" said the wind, and tried to pull his hat off again. "Do you good! *Whoooo-ooo-ooo!*"

Little black bibs

There was once a flock of young sparrows who were very hungry in the winter. Snow was on the ground, the puddles were frozen, and the trees had no berries left on them. So there was nothing to eat or drink.

Old Dame Kind-Heart saw them looking very thin and miserable one day. So she made a fine pudding of millet seeds, crusts of bread and old biscuits. "This will feed those young sparrows well!" she said to herself. "I'll make a pudding like this each day, and feed them all."

So the next day she rang a little bell and all the sparrows lined up ready for their meal.

"Girls first, and boys after," said Dame Kind-Heart, who was very strict about manners.

So the girl-sparrows lined up and hopped in at the window one by one, pecking up the spoonful of pudding that Dame Kind-Heart offered them.

Then the boys came, and they gobbled up their share too. The line of sparrows seemed never-ending. The pudding didn't last till the end of the line!

"Dear me! Who would have thought there were so many young sparrows?" said Dame Kind-Heart. "I must make a bigger pudding tomorrow."

She didn't know that after they had all had their turn, the girl-sparrows lined up behind the boys, and then when they had had *their* turn, the boys lined up behind the girls again!

You see, both boy and girl-sparrows were exactly alike, so poor Dame Kind-Heart couldn't possibly know which were which. She just thought there must be an extraordinary number of boy-sparrows, coming along in a never-ending line after the girl-sparrows had been fed!

But her next door neighbour, Mister Sharp, told her of the trick that was being played on her, and she was cross.

"Naughty little things," she said. "Well, I will make sure it doesn't happen again!" And that night she got out a pot of black paint, cleaned a little brush and set them ready for the morning.

In the morning, when the sparrows lined up again, she called to them. "Fly into my room for a minute please, boy-sparrows."

When they were all inside, Dame Kind-Heart dabbed a bib of black paint under the chins of all the surprised boy-sparrows. "There!" she said, "now I shall know the girls from the boys! The girls have no bibs – but you boys have little black ones. You can't trick me any more!"

They couldn't, of course, so each sparrow had his or her share of the pudding, and no more. It was quite enough for them too.

The funny thing is that the cock-sparrows still wear their little black bibs, and the hens have none. Do look and see, when next you go out in the garden.

The little thimble-plant

Natalie was very good at sewing. "It's in the family!" her mother told her. "Your great-granny embroidered so beautifully that the Queen of England bought some of her work. And you know how well your granny sews."

"Yes – and so do you, Mummy!" said Natalie. "I'm sure no one can make dresses as well as you can!"

Natalie had a beautiful silver thimble. Her great-granny had used it, and her granny had given it to Natalie when she saw that her little granadaughter was going to sew beautifully.

"Here you are," she said. "My mother used it when she embroidered the tablecloth that the Queen bought. You shall have it. She always said that it had magic in it, because she never sewed so well as when she wore that little thimble!"

Natalie always used the silver thimble. It fitted her middle finger exactly, and shone brightly as she pushed the needle in and out of her work. She often wondered if there really *was* magic in it!

Natalie was fond of gardening as well as sewing. She embroidered flowers on cushions, and she loved to copy her own flowers with her needle and coloured cottons. She had the prettiest little garden, full of candytuft, poppies, marigolds and roses.

"You must go in for the flower show this year," her mother said. "Do you know what the prize in the children's section is, Natalie? It's a work-basket! You need a new one, a nice big one. Wouldn't it be lovely if you could win the prize and take home a big new work-basket!"

"Oh, *yes*," said Natalie, delighted. "I'll grow some lovely flowers in my garden and take them to the show. Is the work-basket to be awarded for any special flowers, Mummy?"

"It's for the prettiest and most unusual plant that is flowering in a pot," said her mother. "You could put one of your garden plants into a pot and show that. You have one or two really unusual poppies. Those double red ones with pink stripes are the prettiest I have ever seen. You would be sure to win a prize with those."

Natalie took her sewing into the garden and sat down by her little garden. She looked at it as she sewed. As Mummy said, those red poppies striped curiously with pink might win a prize.

"It really would be fun to bring home that work-basket," said Natalie to herself. "Now, I'll just finish this bit of sewing, then I'll water my garden. It looks very dry."

She finished her sewing, left it on the grass and went to water her garden. The thirsty earth drank up the water thankfully. Natalie pulled up a few weeds, then gathered up her sewing things and went indoors.

But that evening, when she was showing her mother her sewing, she missed her little silver thimble! "Oh dear – where is it?" she said, hunting in her sewing-bag. "Oh, Mummy, I must have left it out on the grass. I'll have to go and look for it. It's still light."

So out she went. But although she hunted through every blade of grass by her garden she couldn't find her silver thimble. She went back to the house, upset.

"It's gone," she said. "Mummy, could anyone have taken it? Nobody comes into the garden, do they? I'm sure I left it down by my garden. But it isn't there now."

Mummy went to look too, and then they turned out the sewing-bag again.

They hunted all over the floor, and down the garden path. But the silver thimble didn't turn up. Natalie was worried.

"Oh, Mummy, I'm sure that was my lucky thimble. I do hope my good luck won't go now I've lost Granny's magic thimble. She always said it had magic in it. I'm sure it had, too. I could always do my best sewing when I was wearing that."

Well, it was a very strange thing, but it did seem as if Natalie's good luck disappeared with her silver thimble. First she fell off her bicycle and hurt her right hand so that she couldn't sew for a week. Then the dog got hold of the new cushion cover she was making for her mother and bit a hole in it. Then she lost one of her school books and got a scolding.

"If only I could find my silver thimble, I'm sure I'd be lucky again," she told her mother.

"Oh, nonsense," said Mummy. "It's

nothing to do with your thimble. Everyone has bad luck at times. I expect yours has finished now. You'll get a bit of good luck instead!"

But her mother was wrong. Three days before the flower show, just when Natalie's garden was looking really beautiful, two sheep wandered in at the back gate and ran all over the lawns and beds. One found its way into Natalie's garden and ate almost every plant in it!

Natalie ran crying to her mother. "Mummy! There's more bad luck! Those sheep, look – one has eaten nearly everything in my garden. My beautiful poppies – I can't possibly enter them for the flower show now. I haven't a chance now of winning that lovely work-basket!"

Mummy was very sad for her. She shook her head when she saw the spoilt garden. The sheep had been chased back to their field – but oh, what a lot of damage they had done! What a pity to spoil all Natalie's lovely flowers!

"Poor Natalie," said Mummy. "Never mind, darling. Nasty things do happen. You just have to make up your mind not to be upset too much. I've always noticed that if you make the best of bad things, something good comes along sooner or later!"

Natalie was very sad. She took her sewing down by her poor spoilt garden and began to embroider poppies on a new cushion-cover. "And if the dog gets this one I really will shout at him!" she thought. "Oh dear – I've got to use this horrid little pink thimble instead of my own lovely silver one. *Where* did it go, I wonder? Is somebody else wearing it now?"

A little robin hopped down beside her to watch her. Natalie called him *her* robin because he always came to watch when she gardened. She spoke to him and he cocked his head on one side, listening.

"I'm sad because my luck has

disappeared with my little silver thimble," she told him. "I did love it so. Robin, *you* haven't seen it, have you? Do you know who has got it? Did it go down a worm-hole – and is the worm using it for a hat?"

That idea made her laugh. The robin listened, and then gave a sudden little trill and flew into the nearby hedge. She heard him singing loudly, almost as if he were telling somebody something. Natalie wished she could understand what he was singing.

And then a most surprising thing happened. Out from the tangle of weeds in the hedge peeped a small face with bright green eyes, and a very long beard. The face wore a pointed hat on its head, and it looked rather worried.

Natalie stared in surprise. Was it a doll? No, it couldn't be – the face was too small. Besides, it moved. It smiled! And then the face moved forward and a whole body appeared, as somebody came through the weeds.

It was a brownie – such a small brownie that Natalie thought he could live in her doll's house with ease. He came right up to her, the robin fluttering behind.

"You're Natalie, aren't you?" said the brownie, his long beard waving round him in the breeze. "The robin told me. And he said you've lost your silver thimble and you're very upset."

"Yes. I loved it," said Natalie. "Do you know where it is? And are you a brownie? I've seen pictures of brownies in my books, but I never thought that one lived just under my hedge!"

"Children aren't as kind to little creatures as they should be," said the brownie. "So we hide away now. But we're always about. The robin told me you were kind, so I'm not afraid to come and speak to you. And I'm really very, very sorry – but I'm afraid *I've* got your thimble. At least, I think it must be what you call a thimble, though I've never used one myself."

"But why did you take it?" asked Natalie gently, afraid of scaring him.

"I found it halfway down a worm-hole," said the brownie. "I heard the worm complaining because he couldn't get out. It was stopping up his way, you see. So I dragged it out and took it home. I didn't know it belonged to you."

"What did you do with it?" asked Natalie, feeling really excited.

"Well, to tell the truth, I thought it was a plant pot," said the brownie. "Silly of me – but I honestly thought it was. So I planted a seed in it to grow and stood it on a little wooden stand on my window-sill. I'll let you have it back at once, of course."

"Oh, please do!" said Natalie, delighted. "I don't mind your having had it for a plant pot at all – if only you'll give it back to me now. I'll give you this little *pink* thimble if you like, for a plant pot."

"Now that's *very* kind of you," said the brownie, and darted off at once.

He came back with Natalie's silver thimble. He carried it upside down, of course, fitted into its stand because to him it was a pot. In it grew a tiny plant with pretty, feathery leaves.

"What have you planted in my thimble?" asked Natalie.

"It's a wing-flower," said the brownie. "Its flowers are just like fairy-wings, you know, in fact, some fairies cut them off and use them for a spare pair. They only need a spell in them to make them fly."

Natalie looked down at the tiny plant in wonder. It had a nice fat bud at the top! Would it flower into tiny fairy-wings? Oh, how wonderful!

"Thank you. I shan't take out this magic little plant till it dies," said Natalie. "Fancy, it's so small that it grows in a thimble! I shall wait and see if it flowers into wings. Look, here is my pink thimble for you. Come and talk to me again sometime. I'll send the robin to call you when I am here all alone."

"I'd like that," said the green-eyed fellow, and nodded his head. "Thank you for the pink thimble. *I* think it's prettier than the other. Goodbye!"

Natalie took the thimble-plant to her mother. How marvellous! What a wonderful thing to happen!

Mummy could really hardly believe it. She looked closely at the tiny plant. "I have *never* seen one like it before," she said. "Oh, Natalie, you ought to show it at the flower show! It's quite perfect. It should be in flower then, too!"

Well, on the day of the flower show the little thimble-plant burst into flower – and to Natalie's great delight the flower was in the shape of fairy-wings, two dainty blue and silver wings, quivering on the stalk.

"It *is* a wing-flower," said Natalie. "Oh, Mummy, if only I was small enough to fly with them! When the flower dies I'll cut off the wings and fasten them to a little dolls' house doll – *she* might fly with them at night!"

She took the thimble-plant to the show. Everyone exclaimed in wonder when they saw such a strange little plant, with tiny wings quivering at the top of the stalk.

"Wonderful! Marvellous! Where did you get it from?"

Natalie whispered her tale to the children, but she didn't think the grown-ups would believe her, so she didn't say anything to them. The children crowded round the thimble-plant, holding their breath in case they damaged the fairy-wings growing at the top.

Well, of course, you can guess who got the prize. Natalie! She would have got the prize for her poppies, if she had shown them, so she really only got what she deserved. But how pleased she was! Mummy carried the big work-basket home for her, and Natalie carefully carried the strange little plant growing from her silver thimble.

She cut off the wings when the flower

seemed dead, though they were still exactly like proper little wings. And, at the foot of the flower, was a tiny ball of seeds – seeds so fine that they seemed almost like powder.

I wish Natalie would give me one. I *would* so love to grow a wing-flower in a silver thimble, wouldn't you?

Funny little Shorty

B obby brought a new toy home with him one night. He put it in the toy cupboard.

"There you are, little cat," he said. "Make friends with all my other toys!"

He shut the cupboard door and went off to bed. The toys stared at the new toy in silence. What would he be like?

"Hallo!" said the new toy. "Let's go out and have a run round the playroom, shall we? I'd like to see my new home."

They all went out into the big playroom. It was a nice place, with rugs over the linoleum. "Ha, good!" said the new toy, and he gave a little run and then slid all the way along the slippery linoleum on his four black legs.

"You don't do things like that until we know you better," said Rosebud, the big doll.

"Oh dear – sorry!" said the new toy, and he sat down on the nearby rug. "How long will it take for you to know me better? There's not much to know about me, really."

"What are you?" asked the pink rabbit.

"Well – can't you see! I'm a cat, of course," said the new toy.

"You're not," said the toy dog at once. "You haven't got a tail. All cats have tails."

"Not the kind of cat I am," said the cat. "I'm a Manx toy cat – and Manx cats don't have long tails."

"I don't believe you," said the toy monkey, swinging his lovely, long tail. "You're just saying that to make us think it's all right for you not to have a tail. You must have lost your tail somewhere. Don't tell stories!"

"I am *not*," said the little Manx cat,

151

crossly. "I never tell stories. I'm telling you the truth. I'm a little Manx cat, and Manx cats don't have tails – or only just a stump, like mine. Do believe me."

But they didn't. They only laughed at the little toy cat. "We shall call you Shorty, because your tail is so very, very short that you almost haven't got one," said the monkey. "You look silly, Shorty. You ought to try and get a tail somewhere. One like mine!"

"I don't want a tail," said Shorty. "I should feel strange with one. I tell you I'm the kind of cat that doesn't have one. So, I don't want one. Is there a teddy bear here? Yes, I can see him. Well, he hasn't got a tail either – but you don't laugh at *him*."

"No, because he's not *supposed* to have one, so he looks all right without one," said the toy dog, wagging his tail to show how strong it was. "You just look silly without one. All cats have tails."

Shorty gave up. "All right," he said.

"Have it your own way. But let me tell you this – I think you're all rather silly and very unkind. I do think you might be more friendly to a new toy."

But the toys weren't nice to Shorty. They turned away from him and wouldn't show him round the playroom. They didn't talk to him much either, and they never asked him to join in their games. He was very sad about it.

"I can't help not having a tail," he thought. "What difference does a tail make? I wish I lived in the Isle of Man where it's strange for a cat to *have* a tail. Oh well – I must just make the best of things."

So Shorty didn't quarrel or grumble. He was always cheerful and smiling and willing to do anything for anyone. He was even glad to wind up the clockwork mouse when the others got tired of it.

"It's a pity you haven't a long, long tail like mine, Shorty," the mouse said each time the toy cat wound him up. "You do look odd, you know."

"Rubbish!" said Shorty, cheerfully. "There you are – your key won't turn any more, so you are fully wound up. Run along."

Now one day a really dreadful thing happened. A little girl came to tea with Bobby, and they quarrelled. Bobby wouldn't let her take his mother's scissors from her work-basket and use them to cut pictures out of his books.

"No, Jennifer," he said. "For one thing I'm not allowed to have those scissors, and nor are you. And for another thing I won't let you spoil my books. You spoil your own, I know – but I *like* my books."

Jennifer was angry. She was a spoilt, loud-voiced little girl, and she shouted at Bobby.

"You're a meanie, that's what you are! A MEANIE! I don't like you. I'll break your train!"

"No, you won't," said Bobby, and he took his train and went into the bedroom. He locked it up in a drawer and came back. While he had gone Jennifer had run to the work-basket and taken the scissors. Her mean little eyes gleamed. She would pay Bobby back for doing that!

"Go and see what the time is," she said to Bobby. "I think it must be getting late."

Bobby went down to the hall to look at the big grandfather clock there. He hoped it *was* getting late, then this horrid girl would go.

Jennifer waited until he was out of the room, then she ran to the toy cupboard and opened it. She pulled out the monkey, the toy dog, the clockwork mouse, the little kangaroo that could jump, and the lovely little horse with his long, long tail.

And what do you think she did? She cut off all their tails! Then she stuffed the toys back into the cupboard, and put the tails in her pocket. She heard Bobby coming back and hurriedly put the scissors into her pocket too. The

155

sharp end stuck into her and hurt her. She began to cry.

"What's the matter?" said Bobby. But Jennifer couldn't tell him, of course. She just said she wanted to go home, and off she went, wondering what Bobby would say when he saw his spoilt toys.

Bobby didn't see them that evening – but, oh dear, what an upset there was when the toys streamed out of the cupboard that night! How they cried.

Shorty was very sorry for them all, because he knew how much they thought of their tails. He tried to comfort them.

"Cheer up. Perhaps we can make other tails, just as nice as yours. Don't cry."

"Don't be silly," said the monkey. "Where can we get new tails!"

"I can find *you* one," said Shorty, and he pointed to where the curtain was looped back with a long silk plait. "A bit of that would look fine on you!"

"So it would," said Monkey, wiping his

eyes. In a trice Shorty had snipped a piece off the curtain loop, and had given it to Rosebud to sew on to Monkey.

"Find me a tail, find *me* a tail!" begged the little clockwork mouse, running up to him.

"There's a very nice piece of black string in the string-box," said Shorty. "It would make you a wonderful tail!"

And it did. You should have seen the clockwork mouse with his new black tail. It was even longer than his old one.

Shorty was very clever. He found an old furry collar belonging to Rosebud the doll. She said she didn't want it, so he carefully cut it up into two pieces, and made tails for the toy dog and the kangaroo. They were simply delighted.

"My new tail wags better than the old one," said the toy dog and he wagged it.

"What about me, please, Shorty?" neighed the little horse. "My tail was so beautiful – it was made of hairs, you know."

"Yes, I know," said Shorty, thoughtfully. "Now, let me see – what would be best for *your* tail? Oh, I know! What about taking some hairs from the old rug by the fireplace?"

So he pulled twenty hairs from the rug and neatly tied them together. Then Rosebud sewed on the new tail and the little horse swished it about in delight.

"You're very, very kind," said the monkey, in rather a small voice.

"Yes, you are," said all the toys.

"You've bothered about new tails for us," said the toy dog, "but you haven't even *thought* of one for yourself. We've teased you and teased you – and instead of being glad when we had no tails, like you, you were sorry and made some for us. Do, do make yourself a tail, too."

"No, don't," said Rosebud, suddenly. "I like you without a tail, Shorty. I do really. You wouldn't be Shorty if you had a tail!"

"But wouldn't you all like me better

158

with one?" said Shorty, surprised. "I *could* make one, of course. I just didn't think of it for myself."

"No, Shorty, no!" cried all the toys, and the little kangaroo came and hugged him. "We like you as you are. It's funny – but you look *nice* without a tail. Don't have one! You wouldn't be our nice old Shorty!"

Shorty beamed all over his whiskery face. "All right," he said. "I won't have one. I don't want one, because I'm not supposed to wear a tail, anyway! Well – are we all going to be good friends now?"

"Yes – if you'll have us," said the pink rabbit, looking rather ashamed of himself. "And listen, Shorty, if anyone is ever unkind to you again, just go and pull his tail!"

"All right," said Shorty, with a grin. "But I shan't need to!"

And he didn't, of course. They were all good friends after that – but Bobby *is* puzzled about all the new tails!

The naughty little
blacksmith

There was once a lovely village on the borders of Heyho Land called Comfy. The village of Comfy was exactly like its name. All the houses were snug and comfortable, the gardens were fine and grew everything well, and the people were friendly and happy.

So you can guess that plenty of people wanted to go and live in Comfy! But no one was allowed to unless they had work of some sort that they could do.

When Gobo wanted to live there the chief of the village said to him, "What work can you do?"

"I can bake pies and cakes and tarts,"

said Gobo. "I've brought one of my pies with me. Try it."

So the chief tried it and found it very good. "You can come and live here," he told Gobo. "Work hard and make cakes, pies and tarts for us, and you will be very happy."

Another time a rich gnome called

Smug wanted to buy one of the snug little houses. When the chief of Comfy asked him what work he could do, he answered in a very high and mighty voice, "Work! I don't need to work! I've plenty of money without working."

"Well go and spend it somewhere else," said the chief. "People are only really happy when they have work to do, and we don't want anybody here who will not work."

So the rich gnome had to go away, disappointed and angry. The chief of the village watched him and laughed.

"He is lazy!" thought the chief. "A little work would do him good and make him happy. Well, well – we don't want people like Smug here, that's certain!"

Now one day a small pixie called Tiggle came to ask if he might live in the village. The chief came to see him and to ask him questions. Tiggle was very well dressed. He looked cheeky and vain.

"What work can you do?" asked the chief.

"Oh, anything!" answered Tiggle.

"What do you mean by 'anything'?" asked the chief.

"Well – just anything!" said Tiggle cheekily.

"We want a smith – can you shoe horses?" asked the chief, looking at Tiggle's soft white hands and thinking that they didn't look as if the pixie had ever done any work at all.

"Oh, yes, I can shoo anything!" said Tiggle. "I can shoo horses and donkeys and geese and flies – I'm very clever I am!"

"Well, you can come and live in our village then," said the chief. "But mind you work hard!"

So Tiggle moved into a dear little house, well built and comfortable. He hung blue curtains at the window, put soft carpets on the floor and a most comfortable armchair for himself by the parlour fire. Everyone came to give him a hand, for the folk of Comfy Village were the kindest in all Heyho Land.

Tiggle soon settled down and was very happy. He had plenty of money to spend, he kept a little servant, and he made a great many friends.

Whenever the chief of the village was anywhere near, Tiggle would sigh and say, "I've worked so hard this week! I've shooed three geese, four ducks, five hens, and ever so many flies."

So people thought he made shoes of all kinds and said he must be a very clever fellow. But the chief of the village still kept looking at Tiggle's soft white hands, and wondered how anyone could have hands like that if he really did such a lot of hard work.

"I'd like to see the shoes you make, Tiggle," said the chief one day. "I'll come along and see some tomorrow. I've a duck with a lame foot – perhaps one of your shoes would do for it."

Well that gave Tiggle a great shock for, as you may guess, he had never shoed anything in his life. He said goodbye very quickly and caught the next bus to the town over the hill. There he spent a good deal of money on red, yellow, and blue shoes of all kinds. He put them into his bag and went home. He arranged all the shoes in his parlour and the next day when the chief of Comfy came knocking at the door he found Tiggle busy sewing a button on a shoe.

"Dear me!" said the chief, looking all round. "What a lot of shoes! I like this little blue pair!"

He picked up the blue shoes, turned them upside down and looked at them. On the sole was stamped the name of the shop where Tiggle had bought the shoes! The chief put down the shoes and looked at Tiggle, who was still busy with the button.

"So you made all these shoes, Tiggle?" he said.

"Yes, sir," said Tiggle, most untruthfully. He went very red and hung his head over the shoe he was holding.

"Really?" said the chief, and he walked to the door. "Well, tomorrow I'll bring a few things for you to shoe, Tiggle. And I shall be sorry for you if you can't do the job!"

The next morning Tiggle got such a shock – for up the hill to his house came a great crowd of people! The chief came first, leading his lame duck. Then came others, some with a horse, some with a dog or cat, some with hens and geese!

The chief knocked on Tiggle's door. "Come out, Tiggle!" he cried. "We want to see you do some work. We've brought a few creatures for you to shoe!"

Tiggle opened the door and looked at all the animals. "I can't work today," he said. "I don't feel well."

Everybody crowded into Tiggle's little garden. Somebody's goat began to eat the flowers, and the hens scratched up a bed of lettuce.

Tiggle saw them and was very angry. "Take your horrid creatures away!" he shouted.

166

"Not till you've shoed them all," said the chief. "You said you could shoe anything, Tiggle. Was that true?"

"Yes, quite true," said Tiggle sulkily. "But I didn't mean what *you* meant, that's all. I *can* shoo anything!"

"You're not telling the truth," said everybody.

The goat ate all Tiggle's sweetpeas and began on the tomato plants. Tiggle was dreadfully upset, and very angry indeed.

"I *am* telling the truth!" he shouted. "I'll show you! *I'll* show you! Watch me shooing the goat, to start with!"

Tiggle rushed at the alarmed goat, waved his hands at him, and yelled loudly. "Shoo, Goat! Shoo, shoo, SHOO! Shoo, Goat!"

The goat shooed in fright. He jumped right over the wall and ran down the street. Everyone stared with wide open eyes and mouth. Tiggle shouted at them.

"Well, didn't I shoo the goat? Didn't I?

Now I'll shoo all the other creatures you brought to be shoed! Shoo, Duck! Shoo, Hen! Shoo, shoo, all you geese! Ah, you bad creatures, you've eaten my carrots. Shoo, I tell you, shoo! And shoo, you dogs and cats; and shoo, you silly horse, eating my grass. SHOO!"

All the animals and birds fled in fright. They jumped over the wall, squeezed under the gate, flew over the hedge – anything to get away.

"Now stop this, you bad pixie," said the chief, very sternly. "You deceived us. You didn't deserve to live in our happy little village. You . . ."

"I won't be talked to like this!" shouted Tiggle, who was in a fine old temper now. "Shoo, all of you! Shoo! SHOO! I said I could shoo anything, and so I can. I'll shoo the lot of you. Shoo! SHOO!"

"Ho, ho! So that's how you are going to behave, is it?" cried the chief, losing his temper too. "Well, *we* can do a bit of shooing too!"

He slipped off his shoe. Every one else took off a shoe too, and grinned. They knew what was coming.

"Shoo, Tiggle, shoo! Shoe! Shoe!" cried the chief, and he lifted his shoe and gave Tiggle such a smack with it that he jumped high in the air and howled with pain. "How do you like our way of shooing, Tiggle? Shoo, shoo!"

Everyone tried to get in a smack at bad little Tiggle, and cried, "Shoo! Shoo! Here's a shoe for you! Shoo, shoo!"

Tiggle ran down the path to the gate. Shoo, shoo! The goat peeped over the wall and laughed. The geese cackled loudly. Tiggle yelled and shouted, and ran as fast as he could out of the gate.

"It doesn't pay to be deceitful!" cried the people after him. "You'd better be honest next time, Tiggle! Shoo, shoo, shoo!"

Tiggle caught the next bus, crying big tears down his nose. "I was silly," he sobbed. "I daren't go back. I've lost all my goods and left my money behind. Now I shall really have to go to work."

Well, it didn't do him any harm. He went to help a blacksmith, so he really *is* shoeing something now. Maybe one day he'll go back to the village of Comfy and start all over again, honest and hardworking. But I guess I know what everyone will shout if they see him again. Do you? Yes – Shoo, shoo, shoo!

The little mouse and the squirrel

There was a little mouse who lived in a hole in a ditch. He ran about all night long, looking for titbits everywhere – and one night he went into a cottage and sniffed about for a bit of bacon or a piece of cheese.

Aha! What was this? Bacon rind, smelling fresh and delicious! The mouse ran to it and began to nibble.

But alas! It was a trap; and there came a loud rap as the trap worked, and tried to catch the little mouse. He leapt backwards, but his front foot was caught and badly hurt.

The little mouse squealed and pulled

his foot away. Then, limping badly, he hurried out of the cottage by the hole through which he had come, and went back to the wood.

His sore foot made him feel very poorly. He could not go out hunting for grain and seeds as he used to do. He was hungry and wondered if he could ask help from someone.

By his hole he saw a fat grey squirrel. The squirrel was sitting up on his hind legs, his bushy tail well in the air, nibbling at an acorn.

"Hello, Squirrel," said the mouse humbly. "Could you spare me an acorn? Or could you get me a scarlet hip from the wild-rose bramble over there? I have hurt my foot and cannot go hunting for food. I am very hungry."

"What!" cried the squirrel, in a rage. "You, a mouse, dare to ask a grey squirrel for a favour like that! Of course I shall not get food for you! Do you think I am a servant of mice? The idea of asking such a thing!"

"I do not mean to be uncivil," said the mouse. "It is only that I have hurt my foot and cannot get food."

"Then ask someone else to do your hunting for you!" said the selfish squirrel, and bounded off.

The little mouse sat at the entrance to his burrow and watched the squirrel. It was autumn and the little grey creature was storing away tiny heaps of nuts here and there, so that when he awoke for a few warm days now and then in the winter-time he could go to his hidden stores, have a feast, and then go to sleep again.

He hid some acorns behind the ivy-bark. He put some nuts under a pile of leaves in the ditch. He scraped a little hole under the roots of the oak tree and put four nuts there. He went to the hollow tree nearby and hid seven acorns. He was well prepared for lean days in the winter!

The mouse wished he could go and take some of the nuts – but he could

not move far because of his sore foot.
He lay in his hole and nearly starved.
Then another mouse ran by, and saw
the thin and hungry one.

"What's the matter?" he asked,
running into the hole.

The little mouse soon told him. The
other mouse listened.

"Well, you know," he said, "I would
dearly love to help you, but I have a
large and hungry family, and it is all I
can do to find food for them. It is very
scarce this year."

"I know where plenty of food is!" said
the little mouse eagerly. "Get it for me,
and we will all share it! Look for acorns
behind the ivy-bark, and in the hollow
tree. Hunt under the leaves in the ditch
for nuts, and under the roots of the
oak tree opposite! I saw the squirrel
put some there!"

The other mouse ran off in glee. Sure
enough he found nuts and acorns in
plenty. He carried them one by one to
his own hole, fetched the first mouse,

and helped him along to the hole too. Then, with all the mouse family, the first little mouse ate in peace. Soon his leg was quite well, and he could run about happily once more.

The grey squirrel slept soundly until the month of January, when there was a warm spell. He awoke and went to find the nuts – but alas for him! However hard he looked, he could *not* find anything to eat at all! His larders were empty, each one! He went back to his tree hungry, and slept again.

Then February came, and the sun sent warm fingers into the tree where the squirrel slept soundly. Once again he awoke and came scampering down, hungry as a hunter!

He searched behind the ivy-bark – no acorns there! He hunted in the ditch – no nuts there. He looked in the hollow tree – no acorns to be seen! And last of all he put his little paw in the hole he had made beneath the roots of the oak tree. No – not a nut to be found.

He must go hungry.

"I shall starve!" he said, in fright. And then he suddenly caught sight of the little mouse, who was now plump and sleek. The squirrel called to him:

"Oh, Mouse, you are fat! Let me have a little of your food, I beg you! I am lean and hungry, and I cannot find any of the food I stored away. I must have looked in the wrong places!"

"Last autumn I asked *you* for a little food!" said the mouse, stopping. "But you said no! Why should I help *you* now?"

"You are right," said the squirrel sadly. "I treated you badly. There is no reason why you should not treat me the same."

"Wait!" said the mouse. "There *is* a reason why I should not treat you the same, Squirrel! You and I are not alike! You are selfish and greedy, but I am not. You shall share what I have!"

He brought the squirrel two nuts and an acorn. The squirrel thanked the mouse humbly, and vowed that he would repay the mouse when he found his own stores that he had hidden away.

"I was lucky this winter," said the little mouse, with a gleam in his eye. "I found four heaps of nuts and acorns – one behind the ivy-bark – one in the ditch – one in the hollow tree – and one under the roots of the oak. So I and my friends have feasted well!"

The squirrel listened. At first he was angry, but then he remembered that, after all, the mouse had let him have some food.

"So these are *my* nuts and *my* acorn!" he said. "Well – I deserved to lose them for my greed! Forgive me, Mouse! Next autumn I will store up a larder for you too!"

He kept his word, and now he and the mouse are great friends, and if you see one, you will know that the other is somewhere nearby.

The little brownies' race

"Now come along, come along, come along!" shouted Old Man Smarty. "Where are you, Shuffle, Trot and Merry? I've some goods here ready for you to take to my house!"

Shuffle, Trot and Merry, the three little brownies, were playing a game of marbles in a corner of the market. Shuffle groaned. "Blow! Now we must take his sacks on our backs and walk for miles to his house. I'm tired of it! Why doesn't he give us horses to ride?"

"Because we're cheaper than horses," said Trot. "Come along."

The three little fellows went along to where Old Man Smarty was standing by three big sacks.

"Oh – so there you are, you lazy lot!" he said. "Now see – I've bought all these things at the market, and I want them taken to my house as fast as possible, because Lord High-Up is sending for them tonight, and will pay me a good price."

"It's too hot to walk fast with big sacks like those!" said Shuffle.

"We shan't get there before midnight," said Trot, gloomily.

"Well – I'll do my best," said Merry.

"I'll give a gold piece to the one who gets to my house first," said Old Man Smarty. "There's generosity for you!"

Trot, Shuffle and Merry pricked up their ears at that! A gold piece! That was riches to them.

Sly old Shuffle went over to the sacks at once, and quickly felt them all. Ooh – what a heavy one – and the second was heavy too – but the third one felt as light as a feather! That was the one for him!

"I shall hardly know I've a sack on my

back!" he thought. "I shall easily be the first one at the master's house, and I shall get the gold piece before either of them is in sight! Oho – I'm clever, I am!"

He shuffled off with the very light sack on his back. Then Trot went over to the two sacks left, and wondered what was in them. He stuck a finger into one – it was full of something round and hard – potatoes, perhaps? He stuck a finger into the other and felt something loose and soft – what was it – flour – salt – sugar? He pulled out his finger and sucked it.

"Ah – *sugar*!" he said. "That's fine! I can cut a tiny hole in the sack and wet my finger and dip it into the sugar all the time I'm walking along. What a treat!"

So Trot took the second sack and set off to catch up with Shuffle. Merry whistled a jolly tune and went to the sack that was left. He made a face as he lifted it on to his back. "It's heavy – full of potatoes, I think – and the sellers

181

haven't cleaned the mud off them, either, and that makes them twice as heavy. Well – here goes – I must catch up Shuffle and Trot before they get too far, or I'll not win that gold piece!"

But it was difficult to catch up with Shuffle, even though he was not the fastest walker as a rule – because his sack was so very, very light. Shuffle had no idea what was inside, and he didn't care. He was delighted to have picked such a light load!

"That gold piece is as good as in my pocket!" he thought to himself. "Instead of being last today I shall be first! And will I share that gold piece with the others? No, certainly not! They don't deserve it – I'm the sharpest of the lot!"

Trot was having quite a good time with his sack. He made a hole in it and as he trotted along he kept putting in his finger, getting it covered in sugar, and then licking it off. What a joke, he thought – he was lightening his load and having a feast at the same time!

Merry walked fast, but his load was really very heavy – and then he had the bad luck to stub his toe on a big stone, and that made him limp!

"Just my luck!" he groaned. "I always seem to get the heaviest load and to be last for some reason or other. Look at Shuffle now – he must have picked the lightest sack of the lot – and judging by the way Trot is poking his finger in and out of that sack, it's full of something nice to eat. Oh, my toe! I'll never get that gold piece. I can't walk fast with a sore toe!"

So Merry fell behind, but all the same he whistled a merry tune and had a joke for anyone he met.

Now very soon clouds began to cover the sun, and a wind blew up and made the trees sway to and fro. Then Merry felt a drop of rain on his face and he sighed.

"Now it's going to pour with rain and I shall get soaked. I'd better give up all hope of getting that gold piece!"

The rain began to pelt down, stinging the faces of the three little fellows with their sacks. Shuffle was a great way ahead of the others, and he grinned as he looked round and saw how distant Trot was. As for Merry, he was almost out of sight, he was so far behind.

But, as the rain poured down, queer things began to happen! First of all, Shuffle's sack became gradually heavier. He didn't notice it at first, and then he began to wonder.

"*Is* my sack getting heavy, or am I just imagining it?" he thought. He humped it over his shoulder and groaned. "My word, it feels twice as heavy! Whatever can be inside?"

He walked a little further and then felt that he must have a rest, for the sack was so terribly heavy. He set it down and undid the rope that tied the neck. He put in his hand and felt something soft and squashy. What could it be? The squashy thing was very wet indeed for the rain had penetrated right into the sack. Shuffle pulled it out and looked at it.

It was a sponge! A *sponge*! "No wonder the sack felt so light when the sponges were dry!" said Shuffle, in dismay. "Now they're soaked with rain water and as heavy as can be! What can I do?"

He took all the sponges out of the sack and squeezed them dry, and then began to put them back into the sack again. "But what's the use of that?" he groaned. "The rain is as heavy as ever, and the sponges will soon be full of water again!"

Trot came up and grinned. "Hello, Shuffle – so your load was sponges, was it? It serves you right for picking the lightest load as usual. Now you've got the heaviest!"

"What's in yours?" called Shuffle, annoyed, but Trot didn't stop. No, he saw a chance of winning that gold piece now. He was going quite fast. Also, his sack felt lighter!

In fact, it soon felt so light that Trot stopped in surprise. "What's happening to my sack?" he thought. "It really does feel remarkably light!"

He set it down to see – and, to his horror, he found that the sugar was all melting in the rain! The raindrops had soaked through the sack and the sugar was dissolving into sweetened water – and dripping fast out of the bottom of the sack!

"I ought to get under cover, or it will all be melted away," thought Trot, in dismay. "Why wasn't I sensible enough to remember that sugar melts? I *knew* it was sugar all right! Well, I've outpaced old Shuffle – but if I wait till the rain stops Merry will be sure to catch me up and pass me, and I shan't get that gold piece."

So on he went in the pouring rain, while the sugar in his sack melted faster than ever. But at least he was now in the lead!

As for Merry he still whistled in the

pouring rain, for he was a light-hearted fellow. The rain ran into his sack, down among the potatoes and soon muddy water was dripping out at the bottom. Merry laughed.

"You're washing all the dirty potatoes for me!" he said to the rain clouds above. "Hello – there's Shuffle in front of me – he's very slow today!"

He soon passed Shuffle, who groaned loudly as Merry passed him. "My load is sponges!" he shouted. "And they're four times as heavy as they were now that they're soaked with rain."

"Serves you right!" said Merry. "You picked the lightest sack so that you could win that gold piece!"

The three went on through the rain, and at last came one by one to Old Man Smarty's big house. Trot went round to the back door first of all and set down his sack on the ground.

"Ha!" said the big cook, "so you've brought something for the master, have you? Well, wait till he calls you in to see him. I'll tell him you were the first."

The next was Merry with his sack of potatoes. The cook peered at them and smiled. "Well I never – the potatoes are all washed clean for me! That's a good mark for you, Merry. Wait here till the master sends for you."

Last of all came poor Shuffle, very weary with carrying such a wet and heavy load. He set his sack down and water ran all over the floor.

"Now pick up that sack and stand it outside!" said the cook. "My floor's in enough mess already without you making it a running river. What in the world have you got in that sack?"

But Shuffle was too tired to answer. The cook gave them all some food and drink and they sat back and waited to take their sacks to the master.

The call came at last, and the cook took them in to Old Man Smarty.

"Here's the first one – he came before the others," she said, pushing Trot forward. His sack looked limp, wet and empty. Old Man Smarty glared at it.

"What's this? It should be full of sugar! Where's the sugar, Trot? Have you sold it to someone on the way?"

"No, sir. It was the rain that melted it," said Trot. "I was first here, sir. Can I have my gold piece?"

"Bah!" said Old Man Smarty. "Why didn't you get under cover and save my expensive sugar?" Then he turned to Shuffle. "Shuffle, you were third, so you're out of it. Take that disgusting, dripping sack out of the room. Merry, what about you?"

"Sir, he's brought potatoes – and they're all washed clean!" said the cook, eagerly, for she liked Merry. "He *deserves* the gold piece, even though he wasn't the first here!"

"*I* was first!" said Trot. "*I* won the gold. Give it to me, Old Man Smarty!"

"Very well – but *you* must pay me *two* gold pieces for all the sugar you've lost out of my sack," said Old Man Smarty. "That's what it cost me! So if I give you one gold piece, you have to give me two."

"All right. I won't claim it," said Trot, sulkily. "I should have got the sack under cover." He stamped out of the room in a rage. Only Merry was left.

"You weren't the first," said Old Man Smarty. "But you certainly delivered my goods in a better condition than when I bought them – so I shall award the gold piece for that."

He tossed a shining coin to the delighted Merry, who went off to the kitchen with his sack of potatoes. What sulks and grumbles met him from Shuffle and Trot! He clapped them on the shoulder. "Cheer up – we'll go and spend my gold piece together. What's good luck for but to be shared!"

They all went out arm in arm and the cook stared after them. "You deserve your good luck, Merry!" she called. "And what's more, you'll always get it – a merry face and a generous heart are the luckiest things in the world!"